The operation completed, Vilmsky stepped forward with two handkerchiefs, folded bandage-wise, in his hand.

'What are those for?' asked Biggles politely.

'It is customary to blindfold—'

'Forget it,' Biggles interrupted him curtly. 'I always like to see where I am going.'

Vilmsky bowed. 'As you wish,' he said.

The escort fell in on either side of the prisoners, and at a word of command the party moved forward. Down the corridor it marched, and through an open door into a grim-looking courtyard. Across this it proceeded, and came to a halt against a wall on the far side.

Biggles glanced at the sky. It was just turning pink with the first flush of dawn. 'If Ginger is going to do the rescue act, he hasn't got much time left.' He observed calmly.

Algy said nothing. His face was pale.

Captain W. E. Johns was born in Hertfordshire in 1893. He flew with the Royal Flying Corps in the First World War and made a daring escape from a German prison camp in 1918. Between the wars he edited *Flying* and *Popular Flying* and became a writer for the Ministry of Defence. The first Biggles story, *Biggles the Camels are Coming* was published in 1932, and W. E. Johns went on to write a staggering 102 Biggles titles before his death in 1968.

www.kidsatrandomhouse.co.uk

BIGGLES BOOKS
PUBLISHED IN THIS EDITION

FIRST WORLD WAR:
Biggles Learns to Fly
Biggles Flies East
Biggles the Camels are Coming
Biggles of the Fighter Squadron
Biggles in France
Biggles and the Rescue Flight

BETWEEN THE WARS:
Biggles and the Cruise of the Condor
Biggles and Co.
Biggles Flies West
Biggles Goes to War
Biggles and the Black Peril
Biggles in Spain

SECOND WORLD WAR:
Biggles Defies the Swastika
Biggles Delivers the Goods
Biggles Defends the Desert
Biggles Fails to Return

BIGGLES
GOES *to* WAR

CAPTAIN W.E. JOHNS

RED FOX

Red Fox would like to express their grateful thanks
for help given in the preparation of these editions to Jennifer Schofield,
author of *By Jove, Biggles*, Linda Shaughnessy of A. P. Watt Ltd
and especially to the late John Trendler.

BIGGLES GOES TO WAR
A RED FOX BOOK 9780099634416

First published in Great Britain by Oxford University Press, 1938

This Red Fox edition published 2004

3 5 7 9 10 8 6 4 2

The Random House Group Limited makes every effort to ensure that the
papers used in its books are made from trees that have been legally
sourced from well-managed and credibly certified forests. Our paper
procurement policy can be found at: www.randomhouse.co.uk/paper.htm.

Red Fox Books are published by Random House Children's Books,
61–63 Uxbridge Road, London W5 5SA,
a division of The Random House Group Ltd.

Addresses for Random House Group Ltd companies outside the UK
can be found at: www.randomhouse.co.uk

THE RANDOM HOUSE GROUP Limited Reg. No. 954009

A CIP catalogue record for this book is available from the British Library.

Printed and bound in Great Britain by
Cox and Wyman Ltd, Reading, Berkshire,

Contents

Chapter 1

Biggles has Visitors

Major James Bigglesworth, DSO*, more often known as Biggles, turned down the page of the book he was reading and pulled his chair a little nearer the fire. 'Algy,' he announced quietly, 'you're smoking too much.'

Captain the Honourable Algernon Lacey deliberately blew a neat smoke-ring into the air before he replied. 'You think so?' he murmured, pushing his finger through the ring.

'I'm sure of it.'

'What are you going to do about it?'

'The question is, rather, what are you?'

'Nothing – that is, unless you can think of something else for me to do besides twiddle my thumbs in front of the fire.'

'Go to the pictures.'

'And see war-flying as it exists in the fertile imaginations of film producers? No, thank you.'

Biggles turned to 'Ginger' Hebblethwaite, their protégé. 'You know, Ginger,' he said sadly, 'the trouble with some people is they don't know when to stop.'

'I'm getting a bit bored myself,' admitted Ginger, frankly.

Biggles frowned. 'My goodness! Another one, eh? If you

* Distinguished Service Order, a military medal.

7

two feel like that, why don't you take yourselves off and start something?'

'What could we start?'

Biggles shrugged his shoulders. 'Don't ask me. How should I know? If you haven't had enough excitement out of life already, why not go and join an air circus and do a bit of wing-walking, or, maybe, the flying-man act? They're always looking for new fellows to replace those whose parachutes failed to open.'

'What about you?'

'I'll sit in a chair and watch. I've done all the tearing up and down the world I'm going to do for a little while.'

'My nerves are getting worn out with sitting here reading tales in the newspapers about collisions in the air and other horrors,' declared Algy. 'What I need is excitement.'

'What you need is a kick in the pants,' growled Biggles, reaching for his book. He was about to resume his reading when there was a light tap on the door and Mrs Symes, the housekeeper, came in.

'There's a gentleman to see you, sir,' she said.

'Ah-ha!' ejaculated Biggles, tossing the book aside again. 'Who have we here? Is it the answer to your fervent prayer, Algy, I wonder? Who is it, Mrs Symes?'

'He says his name is Stanhauser – or something like that.'

Biggles raised his eyebrows. 'Hm. It sounds as if he might be an interesting sort of a fellow. Show the gentleman in, Mrs Symes.' He rose to his feet to greet the man who, a moment or two later, walked slowly into the room. He was old, not less than sixty years of age, and that he was a gentleman was at once apparent both by his poise and the expression of quiet dignity on his rather sad face. His hair was grey, as was the square-cut beard that

8

covered his chin, but his steady eyes were blue, and as bright as those of a young man. He was dressed entirely in black, with the narrow coloured ribbon of a Continental decoration threaded through his buttonhole.

Biggles took his hat, helped him off with his overcoat, and pulled a chair forward. 'Sit down, sir,' he invited courteously. 'My name is Bigglesworth. These are my friends.'

'Mine is Stanhauser – Max Stanhauser,' returned the other with a rather stiff bow.

'May I offer you a cigarette, sir?' Biggles reached for the box.

'No, thanks; you will pardon my discourtesy, I know, if I smoke one of my own,' was the quiet reply. 'You see,' went on the old man, in explanation, 'my throat gives me a little trouble, so I am obliged to confine myself to a special brand of cigarettes made from pure Turkish leaf. Permit me to offer you one.'

'That's very kind of you – thanks.' Biggles lighted the cigarette and sat back. 'You came to see me, I think?' he prompted.

The merest suspicion of a smile crossed the other's face. 'More than that; I want you to help me,' he answered frankly.

Biggles glanced at Algy, but his face was expressionless. He looked back at his visitor. 'If you will tell me in what capacity I could serve you, perhaps – '

'Very well. I will – how do you say? – put my cards on the table. That will be best, perhaps, for both of us. My name is unknown to you – yes?'

There was just enough accent in the old man's voice to reveal him to be a foreigner.

'I'm afraid I cannot recall having heard it before,' admitted Biggles.

'I am the Maltovian Ambassador in London, and have been for some time.'

Biggles smiled apologetically. 'Maltovia? Forgive me, but my geography is bad. I can't quite place Maltovia.'

'Few people, except those who live in or near that little state, could describe its position precisely on the map, I think. Maltovia is a principality lying slightly to the north-east of the Black Sea.'

'In Europe?'

'Of course, but only just. Still, we can claim to be Europeans, and there is much difference between Europe and Asia, which is not far from our eastern frontier.'

'As you say, there is much difference,' agreed Biggles. 'And what, may I ask, is the trouble in Maltovia?'

'There is no trouble in our country,' was the gentle answer. 'The trouble is outside, but it may presently reach us. Like many another small state, we find ourselves, in these days of aggression, in danger of being absorbed by a larger one. The story is as old as the hills. Greedy eyes are upon little Maltovia. Fortunately, in the past we have been safe from the great Powers because they watch each other so closely, and any move by one towards annexation would at once be challenged by the others. But now we are threatened in – how do you say? – a roundabout manner. On our northern frontier is another state, not large, as countries in Europe go, but larger than we are. I mean Lovitzna. The Lovitznians are our hereditary enemies. They have recently made a secret pact with one of the great Powers, in return for which Maltovia is to be theirs.'

'How do you know that?' asked Biggles quickly.

'We have our sources of information.'

'But surely your ruling prince will have something to say about that?'

10

'At the moment we have no prince, but the Sovereign Princess Mariana, daughter of our late prince, administers our little country with ability and affection.'

Biggles shook his head sadly. 'You need a man in times like this.'

For an instant the old man's eyes flashed. 'We are happy with our princess,' he said softly, 'if others would only leave us in peace.'

Biggles moved uneasily. 'And – er – just what do you think I can do about it?'

'You could be of great assistance to us.'

'In what way?'

'The Lovitznians are preparing for an offensive. We have definite proof of that. They know that we have certain defences that would prove serious obstacles to an invasion. Needless to say, we guard those secrets jealously, but from one direction we are powerless to protect ourselves from observation.'

'You mean—?'

'The sky. Up to the present there has been little flying in our part of the world, which may account for the fact that we now find ourselves in need of pilots. Lovitzna has recently imported some aeroplanes and, secretly, she must have had some pilots trained in the country from which she acquired them. Also, we hear some foreign pilots came with the aeroplanes. Now, every day, they fly over our country, watching, and, no doubt, taking photographs of our defences.'

A frown creased Biggles's forehead. 'But that's a scandalous state of affairs,' he declared indignantly. 'Do you mean to say that you allow the air force of another power to fly over your country without permission?'

A sad smile crossed the old man's face. He raised his hands, palms outwards. 'Allow? Do you think that we

11

should allow them to do that if we could stop them? Now perhaps you understand why I've come to you.'

Biggles shook his head. 'I'm sorry, Mr Stanhauser,' he said quietly, 'but I could not undertake such a job as the one I perceive you have in mind.'

'But you are a great pilot, well skilled in war-flying—'

'I may know something about the business,' interrupted Biggles, 'but it is not a question of ability. I should get into trouble here if I got mixed up in European affairs, possibly lose my licence. In any case, I would rather not get entangled in a continental fracas.'

'Fracas! You call the extermination of a home-loving people a fracas?'

Biggles flushed. 'Forgive me, I didn't exactly mean that,' he muttered awkwardly. 'It was just a comparative term, that's all.'

'To you, Maltovia is – just a small – affair. I see. Perhaps you are right.' The old man rose. 'I am sorry,' he said simply. 'In my heart when I came here was a ray of hope that you would help us.'

'I am sorry, too, but I've finished with war-flying.'

'You have flown in war before.'

'That is true, but it was not quite the same. Then I was fighting for my own country, which is something every man must be prepared to do.'

'Ah, I understand.'

Biggles helped the old man on with his coat, walked with him to the door, and held out his hand. 'Good-night, sir,' he said.

'And good-night to you.' The Maltovian Ambassador walked slowly away.

Biggles returned to where the others were still sitting by the fire. There was a thoughtful expression on his face. 'You know, I liked that old boy,' he said sadly. 'What I liked about him particularly was the way he kept off the question of money. He was too much of a gentleman to try to bribe me.'

'Then why the dickens didn't you say we'll give him a hand?' demanded Algy coldly.

'Because, if you want to know the honest-to-goodness truth, I can think of no sane reason why we should throw our lives away uselessly fighting for people we do not know, a country we have never seen, and are never likely to see.'

'Who says we should throw our lives away?'

'I do. Do you suppose that we three could take on a country already equipped, and backed by a great Power? Don't be foolish.'

Algy sighed. 'I suppose you're right,' he admitted reluctantly. 'I – what the deuce!' He broke off as there was a sharp rap on the door, which an instant later was flung open.

A man stood on the threshold, a middle-aged, clean-shaven, hard-featured man, with a square face on which the cheek-bones were high and prominent. The hair round his ears was clipped close.

'Who is Bigglesworth?' he demanded harshly, with a coarse, guttural accent, and without removing his hat.

Biggles had sprung to his feet at the interruption. Now his lips closed in a grim line as he approached the intruder. 'My name is Bigglesworth,' he said icily. 'Pardon me if my memory is at fault, but I do not remember inviting you to my rooms.'

'I invited myself,' was the curt reply. 'I have come to tell you something.'

'Then perhaps you would say it as quickly as possible.'

'I came to advise you to keep out of other people's business.'

13

Biggles inclined his head slightly. 'I see,' he said slowly. 'By the way, I think you omitted the courtesy of mentioning your name.'

'Zarovitch is my name.'

'And you come, perhaps, from – Lovitzna?'

'Lovitzna is my country.'

Biggles smiled faintly. 'I am pleased to hear it. Then let me give you a piece of advice. I would recommend that you return to Lovitzna with all possible speed before some Englishman gives you a poke on the nose.'

The other's eyes flashed, and his jaw protruded belligerently. 'I am my country's representative in England,' he snapped.

'Then it is a pity your country cannot find you better employment than snooping around following the representatives of other nations,' returned Biggles promptly.

The Lovitznian's mouth set grimly. 'So! You go to Maltovia, eh?'

'Do you – er – mind?'

'I do.'

'Perhaps you would like me to ask your permission?' Biggles's tone was bitterly sarcastic.

The visitor took another pace into the room. A smile played about his lips, but his eyes were cold. 'Listen, young man,' he said. 'I will make you a proposition, a better proposition than the one Stanhauser has offered you.'

'And I'll make you one,' answered Biggles softly.

'What is it?'

'That you get out of my rooms before I throw you out.'

The other forced an ingratiating smile. 'May I ask what it is you don't like about me?'

Biggles reached for a cigarette and tapped it on the back of his hand. 'You may,' he said. 'Since you ask, I don't like

14

anything about you. I don't like your country, I don't like your face, I don't like your manners, and I don't like your name. I trust I have made myself clear?'

The other breathed deeply. 'Yes,' he said, 'you have made yourself quite clear. Perhaps one day I may find an opportunity of making myself – just as clear.'

'Your opinion then, as now, will be a matter of complete indifference to me,' Biggles told him. 'Would you mind closing the door as you go out?'

The Lovitznian bowed ironically. Then he went out and slammed the door.

Biggles turned on his heels. His manner was brisk. 'Pass me the telephone directory, Ginger,' he said crisply.

Algy started. 'What are you going to do?'

'I'm going to ring up the Maltovian Embassy.'

'Why?'

'Why? Why do you suppose?' snapped Biggles. 'I'm going to Maltovia, that's why. You look like getting all the excitement you've been craving for, the pair of you.'

Chapter 2

Disquieting News

Ten days later, shortly before ten o'clock in the morning, the three airmen were seated round a table in the dining-room at Southwick Airport; a fourth place had been laid, but as yet the chair was unoccupied.

Biggles glanced at his wrist-watch. 'We are a minute or two on the early side,' he observed. 'I don't suppose Count Stanhauser will be late.' The airmen had only discovered their visitor's title after he had departed.

'This looks like him coming now,' said Ginger, who was looking through the window at the railway station in which an electric train had just come to a halt. 'Yes, there he is; he's coming across,' he concluded.

The intervening days between Biggles's swiftly formed decision to go to Maltovia and the present had been busy ones, for there had been many matters to occupy his closest attention. Perhaps the most important item had been the choice of equipment they were to use in Maltovia, for the little state possessed no air force and, consequently, no aeroplanes, and it therefore became necessary for them to supply the deficiency. By arrangement with Count Stanhauser, who was, of course, responsible for the finance, the machines Biggles had selected were all single-seaters of a type that had recently become obsolete in the Royal Air Force, the famous Launcester 'Lance', and three of these now reposed in a closed hangar that had once belonged to a now-defunct air charter company.

This was not all. There had been the matter of mechanics, and to fill this gap Biggles had looked up his old war-time fitter*, Flight-Sergeant Smyth, and Corporal Carter his brother-in-law, who had been a rigger** in the RAF. Both men expressed themselves delighted at the undertaking. They had already left for Janovica, the capital of Maltovia, by rail, to make the necessary arrangements for the accommodation of the three aeroplanes on their arrival. Thus the Maltovian Air Force comprised a personnel of five, three officers and two other ranks, with three aeroplanes. It was, as Biggles had told the others at a final gathering, 'small, but what it lacked in size it would have to make up for in efficiency.' Count Stanhauser had replied to the effect that money was now being raised in Maltovia, which would, he hoped, enable the tiny air force to expand in the near future; young Maltovians would be selected for training as pilots, and as soon as they were ready to take their places other machines would be acquired.

There were also such matters as uniforms and national markings for the aeroplanes to be considered. In regard to the former, it had been decided to adopt the regulation Maltovian army uniform of a pale-blue jacket, with a small pair of gold wings on the left breast, and breeches with a red stripe, continental pattern service caps and black field-boots. For identification markings on the machines it had been agreed to use the Maltovian national colours of red, black, and green, but these had not yet been put on for fear of international complications while the machines were being flown across Europe. For the

* A mechanic specializing primarily in aircraft engines.
** A person who looks after the airframe, particularly the adjustment of the control surfaces and wings.

same reason their uniforms had been packed in their suitcases.

The three airmen rose as Count Stanhauser entered the room and walked over to them. Biggles pulled out the vacant chair. 'Well, here we are, sir,' he said, smiling cheerfully. 'All present and correct.'

The Count sat down and Biggles signalled to the waiter to serve breakfast.

'So you are all ready for departure?' questioned the Count.

'Everything is settled as far as we are concerned,' answered Biggles. 'Are your arrangements complete?'

'I think so.'

Biggles raised his eyebrows. 'You only think? That isn't enough, sir. On this job we must always be sure. What are you doubtful about?'

The Count looked uncomfortable for a moment. 'It isn't doubt, perhaps, so much as fear, knowing that so much depends upon this issue,' he said quietly. 'The necessity for landing between here and Maltovia was an unexpected difficulty.'

'No single-seater, even with the special long-range tanks which I have had fitted to our machines, could possibly fly all the way from here to Maltovia without an intermediate landing for petrol,' declared Biggles. 'I told you that, and you said you would make arrangements for us to land in Weisheim, which is about half-way.'

'That is true and I have made such arrangements. You warned me, you remember, that in this matter we should have to be very careful because of the suspicion with which military aircraft are regarded in Europe. Bearing this in mind, I have arranged with a friend of ours in Weisheim, who owns a large estate, to have his private aerodrome ready for your reception, with an ample supply of fuel.'

'What's wrong with that? It sounds an ideal scheme to me,' confessed Biggles. 'You will have to give us the precise position of this aerodrome, of course.'

'I have marked the place on the map which I will give you in a moment. Yet, somehow, I have a feeling of disquiet.'

Biggles glanced at the others. He did not need telling that the Count was holding something back. Turning again, he looked him straight in the eyes. 'Count Stanhauser,' he said in a low voice, 'we all know that by making an unauthorized landing at Weisheim, instead of landing at an official customs airport, we are committing a breach of international regulations punishable by imprisonment; that is a risk we must be prepared to take – if that is what is worrying you. If you are thinking of something else, why not be quite frank with us? By withholding anything, no matter how insignificant it may appear, you must lessen our chances of success.

The old man leaned forward in his chair. His expression was very serious. 'Major Bigglesworth,' he said in a voice so low that it was little more than a whisper, 'I am going to be absolutely honest with you. We have reason to suspect that our lines of communication are being tampered with. It is so hard to know whom we can trust.'

Biggles looked grave. 'You mean that Lovitznian spies are on the job?'

'That is precisely what I do mean.'

Biggles took out a cigarette and tapped it thoughtfully on the table. 'I can't say that I am surprised,' he murmured. 'In fact, I was half prepared for something of the sort. The question arises, how far will they go?'

'They will go to any lengths to prevent the fulfilment of our plans, you may be sure.'

'I don't doubt that. What I really meant was, how acute

19

is the danger? How much does the other side know already?'

'That is a question which, I fear, I cannot answer.'

'But you suspect that there may be a hitch at Weisheim?'

'Frankly, yes.'

'What is the name of the man who owns the place?'

'Baron von Kestler.'

'Have you proof that he is a friend?'

'The Baroness, his wife, is a Maltovian. She has helped us in the past. It was with her, in the absence of the Baron, that I conspired for your landing.'

'Ah!' Biggles was silent for a few moments after his quiet ejaculation. 'Well, we can't hold up things now; we shall have to do the best we can,' he went on. 'What about the position in Maltovia? Is there any reason to suspect treachery or sabotage there?'

'It is hard to say.'

'This is all very vague,' muttered Biggles. 'Can you give us the name of a man there, a prominent man, whom we can trust absolutely? It would be useful to know some one like that.'

'You can trust my nephew, Ludwig Stanhauser, with your life. He knows you are coming.'

'Does he speak English?'

'He was educated in England. It was upon his suggestion that I came to see you.'

'Good! Any one else?'

'The Princess. She has also been to England and speaks your language.'

'We are hardly likely to see her, I imagine. Any one else?'

'It would be better, I think, if you pursued this question with Ludwig. After all, it is some time since I was at home in Maltovia, and things outside my knowledge may have occurred. I only know that there is renewed activity on the part of the enemy.'

'What you really mean is, they know we are coming out?'

'I wouldn't go so far as to say that, but it might be so.'

'What gives you that impression?'

'Zarovitch, the Lovitznian minister in London, has returned to Lovitzna. He went hurriedly.'

Biggles frowned. 'The dickens he has. That doesn't sound so good. Well, we can't do anything about it if he has. Anything else?'

'One more thing I must tell you.' The Count began drawing invisible lines on the tablecloth with a fork. 'General Otto von Nerthold, one of our most able military leaders, a true patriot and the strongest man in our country, an officer to whose zeal we owe our defences, was assassinated last night.'

Biggles caught Algy's eye for an instant before he looked back at the Count. 'That's bad,' he said. 'It looks as if the enemy are going to try to win their war by underhand methods.'

'Such is Lovitzna's way, and the way of the big country behind them.'

'In which case our straightforward methods may cause them some surprise,' answered Biggles grimly.

'Be ever on your guard.'

'It's as bad as that, is it?

'I fear it is. Tell me, are you armed?'

Biggles made a grimace. 'Yes,' he said slowly, 'we are, and it would seem to be as well for us that we are. For risks of war I was prepared, but murder by unseen enemies is unpleasant to contemplate.'

'I would have warned you earlier,' declared the Count

sadly, 'but I did not know that matters had reached the stage they have until I received a dispatch this morning. In fairness to you I must offer you the option of withdrawing if you wish.'

'We don't withdraw when once we have started, sir.'

'It brings joy to my heart to hear you say that.'

'We shall endeavour to be worthy of your confidence,' said Biggles seriously. 'You have no more unpleasant news for us, I hope?'

'No, I do not think that I have anything more to say, beyond once more expressing my deepest gratitude for what you are doing, at the same time regretting that our little country is not in a financial position to recompense you more in accordance with your worth.'

Biggles permitted a faint smile to cross his face. 'We are not doing this for money, Count Stanhauser,' he said quietly. 'If you want the truth, we are doing it because there is in us, as there is in most Englishmen, a love of justice, a sense of right and wrong, and sympathy for the underdog. That is why we shall be proud to wear our Maltovian uniforms.'

Tears sprang to the old man's eyes. He was almost overcome by emotion. 'Yes, ... I knew ... that,' he said huskily. 'Then there is nothing more to say except goodbye, and may God go with you to defend the right.'

Ten minutes later the three 'Lances' took up formation over the aerodrome and, with Biggles leading, headed south-east towards the Channel. Below, on the deserted tarmac, a single lonely figure watched them go, his right hand held high in farewell.

Chapter 3

Dangerous Ground

For nearly five hours the three machines bored their way across Central Europe at a speed of nearly two hundred miles an hour over masses of billowy cumulus cloud that was rolling slowly in the same direction as they were travelling. More than once, when the earth was completely blotted out, Biggles was compelled to go down under the cloud bank in order to pick up a landmark to make sure that he was on his course. A glance at the watch on the instrument-board, and a quick mental calculation, told him that they were approaching their destination, and he expressed his relief in relaxation, for, although he had said little about it to the others, he could not entirely rid himself of the fear of a forced landing, knowing well what the result would be. The machines would certainly be impounded if nothing worse.

Indeed, more than once he half regretted the hasty decision that had sent them out on yet another mission; not for himself, but for the others, Ginger in particular. He himself knew only too well what the future was likely to hold, for he no longer had any delusions about war-flying. Algy knew, too, he reflected, and he was well able to take care of himself; but Ginger was young, and, however well he might be able to fly, real war-flying was something new to his experience. The responsibility was on his shoulders, and if anything happened to the lad who was now roaring along near his left wing-tip, he knew that he would never forgive himself. Therefore doubts assailed him. What would happen if any of them had the misfortune to be forced down in Lovitzna? It was unlikely that they would be accorded the normal treatment of prisoners of war. Caught in arms against another country, it would be useless to appeal to the British Foreign Office for assistance; in any case, his spirit revolted from such a course. Well, time would show. The curious part of the affair was that they were getting nothing out of it. They stood to lose their lives, and against that, to gain nothing – at least, their pay as Maltovian officers, a matter of a few shillings a day, really amounted to nothing. It was always the way when one was fighting for a cause, he thought moodily. Still, it was too late to turn back now.

What sort of reception awaited them at Weisheim, where they were to refuel? He himself had entertained doubts before the Count had amplified them by relating the circumstances of the arrangement. To have the machines confiscated before they so much as reached the country for which they were bound would indeed be a bitter anticlimax. It would not happen if he could prevent it, and to that end he had made certain private arrangements without taking the others into his confidence, the reason for this being that he was anxious not to alarm them.

Another glance at the watch and he throttled back to half-throttle, eased the stick* forward, and glided down into the piled-up vapour above which they had been skimming. In an instant he was swallowed up, but holding the stick steady, in a few seconds he emerged into a dim world, grey in the fading light of the November evening. He was rather sorry about the cloud, for it forced him to

* Slang for control stick or control column; a lever used to control the altitude and movement of an aircraft.

fly lower than would have been necessary had the sky been clear, and, moreover, against the grey background the machines would stand out to watchers below as clearly as flies on a ceiling. Yet there was no help for it; he had never before flown over Weisheim, and only by using his eyes could he hope to pick up the landing-ground, which, the Count had informed him, was marked out with the usual white circle.

A glance over his shoulder revealed the other two machines close behind. They had opened out somewhat in coming through the cloud, so he held on his course just below the 'ceiling'**, watching the ground intently. He was just beginning to get worried when a broad river came into view, and he grunted his satisfaction, for this was the landmark for which he had been waiting. Reaching it, he turned sharply to the left, and after following its winding course for about ten miles, struck off again to the east over fairly open country, scrutinizing methodically every inch of the ground with the thoroughness of long experience. A few minutes later his patience was rewarded when a small white circle, set in the centre of a large, open stretch of parkland, came into view. Not far away to the north the grey pile of a big country house rose above a group of trees. Signalling to the others that he was going down, he throttled right back and glided towards the circle, for, in accordance with their prearranged plan, he was to be the first to land.

His steady eyes regarded the landing-ground with satisfaction, but, at the same time, at the back of his mind there was a vague uneasiness which he could not dispel. Not a soul was in sight, and this, far from allaying his fears, only served to strengthen them. Why was nobody

** Slang: the maximum height to which the aircraft can be taken.

there, he wondered. Their arrival was expected, in which case it was only reasonable to suppose that some one – the Baroness or her servants – would be there to receive them.

As slowly as he dared, he glided on towards the white circle, his whole mind concentrated on the field, its surface and surroundings. At a height of not more than twenty feet he acted as though he was going to land, but at the last moment he turned, and opening his engine, roared low along the boundary of the unofficial aerodrome. Suddenly he caught his breath and stared hard. Had he been mistaken? He crossed the field and raced back along the opposite side. No, there was no mistake. Right across the green turf, at intervals of about fifty yards and not more than two feet above the ground, had been stretched a series of wires. The field had been 'trapped', and any machine attempting to land on it would inevitably turn a somersault. But for the fact that the wire was new it would have been impossible to see it, and even so, had it not been for his particularly careful examination, which would not, of course, have occurred in the ordinary way, the trap would have escaped observation, if for no other reason than that it was hardly to be expected. Biggles's face was grim and slightly pale as he zoomed high to where the others were circling, waiting to follow him in. They closed up, goggles raised, eyes questioning, but he only shook his head and turned away to the north. Glancing down as he sped over the far boundary of the field, he saw something that brought a slow smile over his face: a dozen or more men, most of them in uniform, had run out from a clump of trees and were staring upwards. 'I'd give a lot for the pleasure of shooting you up,' he thought savagely as he regarded them; but then he dismissed the matter from his mind, and set off on a new course, deliberately keeping low so that the men on the aerodrome could not mark his direction. Glancing over his shoulder, he noted with satisfaction that the other two machines were following in their proper places.

It was nearly dark, and he was running on the last of his petrol, the gravity tank*, when a main road appeared ahead. He followed this a little way, and then, choosing a field large enough for a safe landing, he glided in and came to a standstill in the heavy shadow of a belt of trees on the far side. He switched off, and jumped down as the other machines landed.

'What's the idea?' cried Algy, as he and Ginger ran up.

'The field was trapped,' Biggles told him shortly.

It was not necessary to explain to Algy what a 'trap' was; his face expressed his horror and consternation. 'Phew!' he whistled. 'The dirty dogs.'

'How was it trapped?' asked Ginger.

'It was wired to catch our wheels and throw us over as we glided in,' Biggles told him.

'Do you mean to say there are people in the world who would do a thing like that?' cried Ginger incredulously.

Biggles laughed bitterly. 'That's nothing to what some people would do; maybe you'll discover that one day.'

Algy was looking concerned. 'Now we are in a nice mess,' he muttered. 'We can't go on without juice, and I was down to my last pint when you dropped in here. How do you propose to get umpteen gallons of petrol without attracting attention?'

'You'll see.'

'Do you mean to tell me that you think you can?'

'I made provision for that before I left England.'

---

* Usually a small reserve of petrol, held in a tank relying on gravity to feed it through to the engine, rather than pressure or a pump.

'You did? You didn't say anything to me.'

'It wasn't necessary. When I did it, it was merely a precautionary measure.'

'When you did what?'

'I sent a cable to Jerry Banham, in Weisheim. He used to be in 40 Squadron, you remember; he's the Shell Company's agent in this part of the world now. I asked him to bring a load of petrol along this road to-night, and if he saw three machines flying low to follow them as fast as he could. I saw a lorry parked beside the road as we came along; it started off in the same direction as we were going, so I'm hoping old Jerry hasn't let us down. This is him, coming down the road now, I'll bet. Come on.'

With one accord they all ran down the hedge and reached the main road just as a lorry came abreast of them. Biggles let out a yell. The lorry stopped with a grinding of brakes, and a well-dressed man jumped down from the driver's seat.

'What cheer, Jerry?' grinned Biggles.

'Not much,' was the instant reply. 'What do you think you're trying to do – get me the sack?'

'Nothing like that,' Biggles assured him. 'We're in a jam, old lad.'

'What's the trouble?'

'We've got a contract to deliver these machines to Maltovia. Unfortunately, there are some nasty people who don't want them to get there – never mind why. We had a landing-ground fixed up not far from here, but as I was gliding in I noticed that some one had been thoughtful enough to trap it with cross-wires.'

'The low-down skunk!'

'It doesn't matter. I had a feeling that something of the sort might happen, and that was why I sent you the cable. The point is, have you brought us some juice?'

'What do you suppose I came here for – to admire the landscape?'

'Good man! Have you got a hose and a pump?'

'They're part of the lorry.'

'Fine! Then we'll get the machines down here right away.'

'Just a minute,' cried Jerry. 'We don't want to be spotted. I'd better bring the lorry into the field. Can I see the machines up there, under those trees?'

'Yes.'

'All right; go and open the gate, one of you. I'll come up.'

In a few minutes the lorry stood beside the machines, the end of its long hose in Biggles's main tank. By this time it was quite dark, so there was little risk of their being seen.

'How long are you going to stay here?' inquired Jerry.

'Not longer than is necessary, you can bet your life on that.'

'You've got some funny country in front of you; you won't risk it in the dark, will you?'

'Not unless we have to. When we get the tanks full I shall stand by, and if things remain quiet, stay here till dawn. If, on the other hand, people start nosing about, I shall push off and chance it.'

'Good enough; I don't think you can do better than that,' returned Jerry.

Little more was said. In just under an hour the task of refuelling the machines was complete; Biggles paid for the petrol out of his own pocket, and the friend who had stood them in such good service prepared to depart. Ginger went down to the gate, and finding the road deserted, called that all was clear.

Jerry got back on to his lorry. 'Cheerio, Biggles.'

'Cheerio, Jerry, and many thanks.'

The heavy vehicle departed, bumping across the field, and presently the sound of its engine died away in the distance. Ginger rejoined the others, and helped to pull the machines in line, facing the open field ready for a quick take-off should it become necessary.

'Well, that's that,' murmured Biggles, when this had been done. 'We look like having an uncomfortable night, but you can take it in turns to sleep if you like. Personally, I shan't trouble; I shall get away at the first streak of dawn. The sooner we are out of this country the better. I don't like it. The enemy know we are about; there is no longer any doubt about that or the aerodrome would not have been wired. They tried to smash the machines to stop them from getting through, and having failed, they'll try again if they can find an opportunity. It looks as if Stanhauser was right about there being a leakage in his lines of communication, and that isn't going to make life any easier for us. Well, maybe we shall be able to show them a thing or two; we shall see.'

Chapter 4

An Unwelcome Reception

The night passed slowly, and not without anxiety, for more than once cars raced up and down the road, and there were other signs, such as distant calls, which suggested that a search was proceeding. At such times the airmen got into their cockpits, fingering their self-starters, ready to take the air the moment danger threatened. This did not materialize, however, and the hours went by without any one coming into the field in which they had taken refuge. None of them slept or attempted to sleep; in the circumstances they preferred to keep awake. In the early hours of the morning the sky cleared and the moon came up, flooding the world with its pale radiance.

Biggles looked at his watch for the hundredth time. 'It's nearly five o'clock,' he announced. 'I reckon it will start to get light within the next hour, which means that if we took off now we should only be night-flying for about an hour or so. I feel inclined to move on.'

'As we've waited so long why not stay until it's light?' suggested Algy.

'Because, in thinking things over, I believe it would be wiser to get across the frontier of this country in the dark. I shouldn't be surprised if daylight saw machines in the air on the look-out for us. Kestler, or whoever it was who wired the aerodrome, seeing his plans miscarry, is almost certain to ring up the authorities and inform them that three strange military aircraft are flying over the country, and then, naturally, and quite properly, machines would be sent up to stop us.'

'Suppose that happens, what will you do?'

'Make a bolt for it.'

'They may open fire on us if we refuse to go down.'

'Yes, I suppose they might.'

'In which case you'd put up a fight, I imagine? Is that why you had the guns loaded?'

'Great Scott, no! Don't be an ass. Do you suppose I want to start another Great War*? I was thinking of Lovitzna, which we shall have to skirt, when I had the guns loaded. I'm not shooting at any one else's machines. No fear. We'd go to jail for life if we were caught, if nothing worse. But there, I don't think we shall have any cause to worry if we leave the ground in good time. If we leave during the next half hour we shall be a long way off by the time dawn breaks.'

'We might lose each other in the dark.'

'I hadn't overlooked that risk. Even if that happened we should probably be able to see each other when it gets light. The course is due east. Keep above six thousand or you may run into a mountain; there's some biggish country ahead of us. Eight o'clock should see us at the River Danube, which runs pretty well at right angles across our course at the point where we ought to strike it. It's the only big river, and therefore unmistakable. Whoever gets to it first had better fly up and down it, over a distance of, say, ten miles, until the others join him. Ten miles should be ample allowance for any possible margin of error, I think.'

The others agreed, and they all sat down on a low bank

---

* Another name for the First World War 1914–1918.

to wait, but they had only been sitting there about five minutes, luckily, as it happened, in silence, when two men suddenly made their appearance near the machines, which were a matter of some fifteen or twenty yards away. Where they came from the airmen did not know; they never did know, although Biggles afterwards declared that they must have come through the belt of trees, or they would have seen them earlier. They were both in uniform, which looked black in the ghostly light, and they ran forward as soon as they saw the machines.

But Biggles was as quick. Slipping on his goggles to hide his face, he nudged the others, and then, his feet making no noise on the soft turf, he crept up swiftly behind the men, who were now talking in low, excited tones. They appeared to be arguing about their best plan of procedure, but finally came to an agreement and with one accord moved up to the nearest machine. One of them raised his foot with the obvious intention of getting into the cockpit.

But this was more than Biggles was prepared to permit. He could not, of course, make an unwarranted attack on the two men, who, after all, were only doing their duty, but he realized that as the machines had been discovered, they themselves had nothing to gain by remaining hidden. 'Halt!' he said, in a sharp, commanding voice.

The two men sprang round as if he had fired a shot, and there was a moment of tense silence as they found themselves staring into the muzzles of the airmen's automatics.

Biggles was the first to move. With the muzzle of his pistol he waved the men away. Once they understood his intention they needed no second bidding; they began walking backwards, but seeing that the airmen did not move, they soon turned and broke into a run. In a few seconds they had disappeared from sight, but not from sound. A loud hail rang through the still night air.

'Come on,' snapped Biggles, 'it's time we went. Off you go, Ginger. You next, Algy.'

As ordered, Ginger took off first, and got away without trouble. Algy followed, and Biggles, satisfied that he, too, was in the air, raced across the wet turf to join them. None of the machines carried navigation lights*, but Biggles, turning east as soon as he was off, soon picked out one of the others by the orange blaze of its exhaust, and headed towards it. Overtaking it, he showed himself to the pilot of the other machine – for in the darkness he could not make out which one it was – and thereafter settled down to the long flight ahead. A few minutes later the two machines flying together saw the flame of another exhaust some distance in front, and this, Biggles realized, must be Ginger, since he had been the first to take off. Flying on full throttle, the two rear machines soon caught up with the first, and having made their presence known, throttled down again to cruising speed.

Thus, they were already together when a pale glow in the sky straight ahead announced the coming of dawn, and shortly afterwards the silver ribbon of the Danube crept up over the misty horizon. Biggles now forged ahead and took up his position in the lead, and in their original formation they held on their course for the next two hours. They were now over wild, inhospitable country, rugged and gaunt, and Biggles knew that they were approaching the western frontier of Maltovia.

By this time they were flying almost directly into the

* Regulation wingtip lights, red on left, blue-green on right, with a white tail light.

glare of the sun, which was well up, and more than once Biggles squinted long and carefully into it between the outstretched fingers of his left hand, for he did not overlook the fact that in approaching Maltovia from the west they were running along the southern frontier of Lovitzna. He did not expect trouble, but he was taking no risks, and it was as well that he did not, for he presently made out a tiny speck high up in the cloudless blue. He studied it long and thoughtfully, as well as the sky around it, as it headed southward on a course that would cross his own. It was much higher than they were, and as yet still so far away that it was impossible to identify the type of aircraft. Still watching it with the concentrated intentness that can only be acquired by long practice, something else caught his eye. It was only a little thing, a mere microscopic flash, gone as quickly as it had appeared, but it told him a lot. He knew that high up above the lone machine was another, possibly several more, for the flash, unmistakable to one who knew, had been the sun glinting on the wing of a banking aeroplane.

He rocked his machine slightly and then looked back.* The others were closing up, both pilots leaning out of their cockpits to watch him. Raising his left arm, he pointed with the forefinger of his gloved hand in the direction of the strange aircraft. Algy's nod told him that he, too, had seen it. This done, he altered his course slightly to the south, directly into the sun, not because he sought a combat but because he wished to avoid one.

There was no proof, of course, that the other machines

* In the days before radios were routinely fitted to aircraft, pilots communicated with each other by moving their planes or by hand signals. Rocking the wings meant the pilot had spotted an enemy plane.

were hostile. Indeed, there was nothing to show that their pilots were concerned with them, or, for that matter, had even seen them, and he hoped that this was, in fact, the case. The last thing he wanted was to be involved in a fight before he had announced his arrival to the military authorities in Maltovia, over the frontiers of which country they should now be passing, although there was nothing to indicate it. Janovica, the capital, lay nearly fifty miles farther on, in the central plain of the little state.

In this wish, however, he was to be disappointed, and it was not long before he realized it. The lone machine was no longer alone. Four others had joined it, and in a rather ragged V formation the five machines had tilted their noses downward and were racing like arrows across the sky on a path that would bring them in front and above the smaller formation.

Biggles bit his lip in vexation. In his heart he had hoped that the machines might turn out to be harmless civil aeroplanes on a cross-country flight, but there was no longer any question but that they were military aircraft, and single-seater fighters at that. Equally plain was their mission, and when, a minute or two later, Biggles made out the brown crosses of Lovitzna painted on the underside of their wings, he knew that a combat was unavoidable. Still, he did his best to escape it, turning still farther south and putting his nose down in a steep dive in a forlorn hope that he might shake the other machines off.

Looking back over his shoulder he saw them coming, taking advantage of their superior height to gather speed; and as he watched them a change slowly came over him. They themselves were over Maltovia; the Lovitznians were, therefore, virtually committing an act of war even before they had fired a shot. They had no right to be over

Maltovia. Again, there were the people on the ground underneath to consider; they had subscribed their little savings to buy the three Lances; what would they think, if they saw them fleeing from the enemy? It might well be that their morale would suffer, with fatal consequences to the little state, and he decided that that must not happen. If the enemy wanted a fight, well, they should have it, and Ginger would have to take his chance if he hadn't enough sense to keep out of the affair.

Half turning in his seat, he pushed up his goggles and attracted Ginger's attention. Vigorously he signalled to him to turn away and make for the south, and, presently, to his intense satisfaction, he saw him go. A glance over the other shoulder revealed Algy, imperturbable, sitting upright in his cockpit a few yards behind his, Biggles's, right-hand elevator. Automatically he pulled up the handle of his synchronizing gear*, and fired a few shots through his double guns to make sure that they were working properly.

At the sound of the reports a new expression crept over Biggles's face. The habitual quiet, almost placid look disappeared, to be replaced by hard, grim lines that drew his lips tight together with the corners turned down. A frosty light glinted in his eyes. His grip tightened on the joystick and he pushed it slowly forward. The nose of the machine went down and the wail of the wind in the wires became a scream. Down, down, down he roared, while the needle of his air-speed indicator quivered slowly round the dial – 250 ... 270 ... 290 ... 300.

Another glance over his shoulder revealed the five machines pouring down behind, one slightly in advance of

---

* A mechanism which allows the machine gun bullets to pass between the propeller blades without hitting them.

the others. On either side of its swirling propeller tiny orange sparks seemed to be dancing, and Biggles knew that the enemy leader's guns were going, presumably trying to intimidate him, since the range was too long for effective shooting. That was what he had waited for; the enemy had fired the first shot, thus proving his intention. Slowly, but very deliberately, Biggles dragged the stick back towards his left thigh, and the Lance screamed upwards like a rocketing pheasant. Back and back he dragged the stick, left foot pressing on the rudder; then, with a swift movement, he pulled it across into his right thigh. Magically, the Lance straightened out, but not for long; a vertical bank and it was round, now behind the five machines, which had scattered in order to avoid collision as they had tried to follow him in the climbing turn. One pilot, obviously a novice to the business, had side-slipped wide, and was turning this way and that in hopeless indecision as he looked for his comrades.

Biggles was not concerned with him; he was looking for the leader, recognizable at close quarters by small, black strut-pennants. He quickly picked him out, in the act of diving on Algy, who was already engaged with one of the others. Biggles was on his tail in a flash, and he knew at once, from the manner in which the leader skidded sideways before he could fire, that he had a war-tried warrior to deal with. He got in a short but ineffective burst as his opponent pulled up in a tight turn, and then had to swerve himself as the *taca-taca-taca-taca* of a machine-gun sounded unpleasantly close to his shoulder. He whirled round, guns blazing at the other machine as it hurtled past him, narrowly escaping collision. Some of the shots must have reached their mark, even if they did not find the pilot, for the machine zoomed wildly in a frantic effort to get clear. It was a bad zoom. The pilot held his nose up for too long, with the result that the machine hung on the top of its stall. Before it could recover Biggles had tilted his machine up, and taking careful aim at point-blank range, fired a long burst. The Lovitznian machine seemed to shiver. A long strip of fabric ripped off its side and went fluttering away; then its nose whipped over and down.

There was no time to see what happened to it, for Biggles could hear shots hitting his own machine. Again he whirled round and saw that it was the enemy leader, who, in turn, had to bank steeply to avoid collision. Biggles acted with the speed that only comes from perfect co-ordination of brain and muscle. His Lance seemed to spin on its axis, as if an invisible cord was stretched between its nose and the tail of the leader's machine. Simultaneously his guns blazed. The Lovitznian soared vertically, turned on to its side, and then plunged downward in a spin. Biggles, taking a quick glance around, caught his breath as he saw a long feather of black smoke across the blue. He looked down, but before he could identify the machine that was falling in flames shots again compelled him to swerve. One of the enemy, with a Lance apparently fastened to its tail, roared past. Its dive became steeper and steeper until it became almost vertical, and Biggles knew that Algy had got his man. Or rather, that is what he assumed, but on looking up he was amazed to see another Lance banking round to join him. Even then it did not occur to him that the newcomer was any one but Ginger, but the imprecation that he was about to mutter at his return died away as the Lance pilot, pushing up his goggles revealed Algy, slightly pale but smiling. 'Great heaven!' thought Biggles as he realized with a shock that the pilot of the Lance which had driven the enemy machine off his tail must have been Ginger. Swiftly he looked down. One of the machines was a crumpled heap on a hillside; the other was climbing back up into the dogfight. It was a Lance.

Biggles shook his head as one who doesn't know what to think, and then examined the sky. The survivors of the enemy formation had disappeared, but presently he made them out, three of them, all heading northward, one much lower than the others and still losing height. Two of the enemy were on the ground, one a twisted heap of wood and canvas, the other a blazing pyre. 'Well, we've announced our arrival all right,' he thought with mixed feelings as he turned his nose eastward, throttling back to allow the others to overtake him.

Ten minutes later Janovica, the City of the Plains, came into view. Skirting it, he made for the southern extremity, where the Count had told him that a landing-ground was being prepared. He saw the customary white circle at once, and, in a corner of the same field, a large white marquee, evidently the hangar that was to house the machines. Four or five figures stood near it.

As he glided down Biggles examined their new aerodrome and its surroundings. In size it was plenty large enough for their requirements, and it lay less than a mile from the nearest part of the city; to the east the ground was open, but on the southern boundary began a forest that rolled away as far as he could see. So much he was able to observe before he flattened out, and a second or two later his wheels touched the short turf. As soon as the machine had finished its run he taxied on towards the tent in order to give the others plenty of room to land; from a safe distance he watched them come in, and when they had joined him, the three machines together continued their way to where a small party awaited them.

Two figures detached themselves from the group and ran out to meet the machines, taking up positions at each of Biggles's wing-tips. They were Smyth and Carter. Biggles gave them a wave of greeting before moving on slowly to the front of the hangar, where he switched off, and jumping lightly to the ground, walked over to where Ginger was preparing to dismount.

'Didn't you understand my signal that you were to keep out of the dogfight?' he inquired coldly.

'Well, I . . . yes, I . . . of course I . . .' stammered Ginger.

'Why did you come back into it?'

'I thought I might be of some use. After all, I've got to start sometime, haven't I?'

Biggles smiled faintly. 'Yes, I suppose you have,' he admitted reluctantly, 'but in future you had better leave these decisions to me. Come on; come on, Algy, let's go and see what's happening here.'

Chapter 5

Doubts and Difficulties

Besides Smyth and Carter there were three people standing in front of the improvised hangar. All were in uniform. One was a tall man, rather past middle age, with a commanding figure and a powerful face in which were set keen grey eyes. He carried a cavalry sabre, and his hands rested on the hilt as he watched with an expressionless face the approach of the three airmen. Judging by the amount of gold braid on his uniform, he was an officer of senior rank. Next to him stood a slim young man, little more than a youth, with a pale, rather delicate face adorned with a tiny black moustache. He alone of the three was smiling a welcome. He also was an officer, but, clearly, a subaltern*. Behind these, at a respectful distance, stood the other, a private soldier. On the road that formed the boundary on this side of the aerodrome a number of civilians had gathered to watch the scene.

Biggles marched smartly up to the senior officer. 'My name is Bigglesworth, sir,' he said. 'These are my friends, Lacey and Hebblethwaite. You were expecting us, I think?'

'Yes,' was the rather curt reply. 'We were expecting you. I understand from the telephone that you have begun to make war already – yes?'

'Yes, that is correct,' confessed Biggles.

---

* Junior officer, below a captain in rank.

'Why do you do this?' was the next rather surprising question. 'Do you seek to get my country into war with her neighbours, which we are so anxious to avoid?'

Biggles stared. 'I'm afraid I don't understand,' he said slowly. 'Any act of war that has occurred was made by these neighbours you seem anxious not to offend. They attacked us over Maltovian territory. What did you expect us to do in such a case – sit still and be shot at? May I ask your name, sir?'

The younger officer stepped forward. 'This is General Bethstein,' he said nervously. 'General Bethstein is the commander-in-chief of the army.'

'I see,' said Biggles quietly, looking back at the older man, who was still regarding him stonily. 'Very good, sir. I will make a written report about this morning's proceedings in due course.'

'I shall expect one, and I will see you again later in the day.' With that the general turned on his heel, and made his way towards a car that was standing on the road, followed by the soldier who was evidently his orderly-driver.

There was a curious smile on Biggles's face, and he rubbed his chin thoughtfully as he watched him go. He turned to the junior officer. 'Can you tell me where I should be most likely to find Lieutenant Ludwig Stanhauser?' he asked.

'I am Ludwig Stanhauser,' was the instant reply.

Biggles smiled and held out his hand. 'Why, that's fine,' he said cheerfully. 'You're the very fellow I want to see. We know your uncle in London very well.'

'Yes, he has told me in his letters all about you,' replied the other. 'May I, on behalf of all true Maltovians, welcome you to our country!'

'Thanks.' Biggles glanced at the car, now speeding

down the road. 'I should have thought that the general might have said something on those lines, instead of questioning our actions,' he suggested. 'He didn't seem over-pleased to see us.'

The young officer sighed. 'He's a difficult man to understand, and his new responsibilities weigh heavily upon him, I fear. He has only just assumed command, following the tragic death of General von Nerthold, of which you may have heard.'

'Yes, I heard about that,' admitted Biggles. 'What are we supposed to do now we're here? I understood that I was to take command of this aerodrome.'

'Surely. Everything has been very rushed, of course, so we have not yet been able to build accommodation for you here. Still, the aerodrome is close to the town, and quarters have been provided for you at the Hotel Stadplatz. It is not our best hotel, perhaps, but it is very good and quite comfortable; moreover, it is run by a man I know well, and has the advantage of being near the aerodrome. It is to take you there and show you your rooms that I have come.'

'Who arranged that?' asked Biggles.

'I did, on the recommendation of my uncle in London, who has left it to me to extend such hospitality as we can offer. I live with my mother, to whom I will later introduce you. You will all come and dine with us sometime, I hope. Is there anything more you wish to do here immediately?'

'No; I should like to get along to the hotel, where we can get into our uniforms and have something to eat. We have had rather a difficult journey, and it is some time since we had our last meal.'

'Good! Then let us go. I have my car here.'

'Just a minute.' Biggles beckoned Smyth and pointed to the hangar. 'Who erected that monstrosity?' he asked.

'Me and Carter, sir.'

'But why in the name of heaven didn't you paint it? The thing can be seen twenty miles away. What did you think you were putting up – a target?'

'No, sir, but we couldn't get any paint. The General said it would cost too much.'

'I see. Well, we've been to some trouble to get these machines here, and I'm not going to put them into that place for the first Lovitznian bomber to blow sky-high. Where are the stores and ammunition?'

'They're inside, sir.'

'Then get them out.'

'Where shall I put them?'

Biggles looked round the aerodrome and his eyes came to rest on the edge of the forest, at the southern boundary. 'Could you let us have some labourers?' he asked Ludwig.

'Yes, I could find you some workmen. For what purpose do you want them?'

'I want some men to work under my flight-sergeant's instructions, to cut a way into that wood and build a rough shelter there. I want a depot that can't be seen from the air. We'll keep everything over there – you can manage that, Smyth?'

'Yes, sir.'

'I will send some men along right away,' promised Ludwig, as he began to walk towards his car, followed by the others. 'What happened this morning?' he asked, as they all got in.

'We were attacked by five machines bearing Lovitznian markings. 'We shot two of them down and the rest retired.'

'Good – good!' cried Ludwig delightedly. 'That's the best news I've heard for months. That will give them something to think about.'

45

'Well, I thought that was why we came here,' declared Biggles.

'Of course. We have got to stop Lovitznian machines from flying over Maltovia.'

'That's what I understood from your uncle. Has Lovitzna declared war yet?'

'No.'

'Why not?'

'I assume that they are not quite ready to go the whole pig.'

'You mean the whole hog, don't you?'

'Yes, yes. That's right.'

'Well, it strikes me as being an extraordinary situation,' murmured Biggles. 'This flying over your country without permission is nothing less than an act of war.'

'I know; that's the absurd part about the whole thing. If we try to stop them I do not see that they can complain.'

'Neither do I,' asserted Biggles emphatically. 'When do their machines come over?'

'Nearly every morning at dawn.'

'And the General understands that we're here to stop them doing it – to drive them back?'

'Of course.'

'He gave me a very different impression just now.'

'He is worried, and does not want to precipitate the war we fear is coming.'

Biggles nodded. 'I see,' was all he said.

The car was running through the streets of the city now, and presently it pulled up before the entrance to a quaint, medieval-looking hostelry, half-timbered, with a number of heraldic devices along the front. A plump, jovial-looking man with a bald head, and wearing a white apron, ran out and opened the door of the car.

'Hello, Josef,' called Ludwig. Then, to the others, 'This,

gentlemen, is Josef, who will take care of you, as his forefathers have taken care of guests for five hundred years or more. He speaks a little English, but not much.'

They all got out of the car and followed the landlord, who, shouting to his man to carry the bags, led the way upstairs to the first floor where he threw open the doors of three adjoining rooms.

'Here you are,' said Ludwig. 'Make yourselves quite at home. I will leave you now while you have some food and a rest after your long journey.'

'Where shall I be able to find you if I need you?' asked Biggles.

Ludwig handed him his card. 'That is my home address,' he said, scribbling something on the back of it with a pencil. 'And that is my telephone number at the barracks,' he said. 'Don't hesitate to ring me up if I can be of service. I will come back later on tonight and have a talk, if I may.'

'Do; there are lots of things I'm anxious to know about,' returned Biggles, as he threw off his jacket and prepared to wash.

'Good-bye, then, for the present.' Ludwig hurried away.

'You eats soon – yes?' asked Josef, beaming.

'In ten minutes,' Biggles told him, holding up his ten fingers. 'Plenty of food; we're hungry.'

Josef grinned understandingly, and bundled off towards the stairs. As soon as he was out of sight Biggles called the others into his room, a large apartment which was furnished as much as sitting-room as bedroom. 'Close the door, Ginger,' he said quietly. 'I'm beginning to understand what the Count meant when he told us to be on our guard,' he continued, when Ginger returned. 'Unless I am very much mistaken, we have enemies in Maltovia as well as Lovitzna.'

'Who are you thinking of?' asked Algy quickly.

'You've got eyes, haven't you? If old – what's his name? – Bethstein was pleased to see us arrive, then I'm a Dutchman. Why, the man could hardly conceal his chagrin.'

Algy stared aghast. 'Great goodness!' he exclaimed. 'If the commander-in-chief of the army is our enemy, then the sooner we get out of this and back to England, the better,' he muttered.

'I wouldn't go so far as to say that – at least, not at this stage,' replied Biggles. 'But of this I am certain. For some reason or other, Bethstein would rather we had not come here, and that being the case, we can't trust him to look after our interests. We haven't been in the country five minutes, but already we are faced with problems that we may find it difficult to answer.'

'Such as?'

'Those machines this morning. How did it happen that they were right on our route? Was that a fluke, do you suppose? It might be, but I don't trust flukes. It is far more likely that they had been sent out to intercept us; if that is so, who sent them? How did the enemy know that we were arriving today? But there, perhaps it's no use worrying ourselves about these things now. Let's get some food inside us. We'll have a conference later on. From now onwards we must wear our uniforms. That, at least, gives us sufficient excuse to carry pistols, and from what I can see we're going to need them before we're through. I'll see you both in the dining-room in ten minutes.'

The meal, served in the raftered banqueting hall, was a great success. A huge log fire blazed in the open hearth, and the genial Josef, who had evidently put himself out to do honour to his guests, waited on them himself. And they did justice to his efforts. The dining-hall was, of course, a public room, but possibly because of the threat of war that hung over the city, there were few visitors, and with the exception of one or two widely separated lunchers, the airmen had the room to themselves.

Biggles yawned as he finished his coffee and pushed back his chair. 'My goodness, I'm tired,' he confessed. 'I feel I could sleep until the cows come home again.'

'I can hardly hold my head up,' declared Ginger. 'It must be the air, or the excitement this morning.'

'Possibly the fact that we didn't get any sleep last night has something to do with it,' suggested Biggles, mildly sarcastic.

'I think a nap would do us all good,' announced Algy; 'I shall be no good until I've had one, anyway.'

'Come on, then,' decided Biggles. 'Let's go and have a rest. We'll forgather again just before tea and have a council of war.'

Several pairs of eyes were on them as they stood up, neat and smart in their new uniforms, and made their way slowly upstairs.

Chapter 6

An Unexpected Visitor

Biggles awoke with a start. With a single movement he sat upright on the bed on which he had been lying. Something had awakened him, he knew. What was it? The room was in darkness, which told him that he must have slept longer than he intended, but how late it was he did not know. Feeling quietly in his pocket, he found a box of matches and struck one. A quick glance around showed him that there was no one in the room, so concluding that he had, after all, awakened in the ordinary way, he moved across to the oil lamp with which the room was provided. He lighted it, and had just replaced the glass chimney when there came a soft tap on his door. There was something almost furtive in the gentle knock, and he knew that it could not have been made by Algy or Ginger, who would have followed up the knock by walking in.

Four quick strides took him to the door, and with a swift movement he threw it open. In the corridor stood an old woman, dressed in black, almost nun-like garments, a basket of flowers over her arm. Behind her stood another woman, but her head was bowed so that he could not see her face. He was about to make signs that he did not want any flowers when, to his astonishment, the old woman, after a swift glance up and down the corridor, laid a finger on her lips. Wonderingly, but alert for danger, he took a step backwards. Instantly he was followed into the room by the two women. With a swift movement, surprisingly swift for one of her age, the old woman placed the basket of flowers on the floor and locked the door on the inside. Wheeling round, her eyes flashed to the uncurtained windows. Quickly, without a glance at Biggles, she crossed the room and drew the heavy curtains.

So quickly had all this happened that Biggles had had no time to speak; or perhaps it would be more accurate to say that he had been unable to find words to frame the protest that rose to his lips at this remarkable and unwarranted intrusion. Moreover, such was his interest that he had not taken his eyes off the old woman. Now, remembering the other, he turned, and inexpressible astonishment surged up in him at what he now beheld.

Facing him, regarding him with an expression of quiet dignity, was a girl. She could not have been more than eighteen years of age, but it was not this that held him speechless. It was her beauty. She was rather pale, but he thought that her features were the most perfect he had ever seen. With a sudden movement she threw back the hood-like garment that covered her head, releasing a halo of golden curls which, with a rather tired gesture, she shook into place. 'Forgive me,' she said softly, and as soon as she spoke Biggles suspected who she was, for there was something regal about her voice as well as in her poise. 'I am the Princess Mariana of Maltovia,' she concluded quietly.

Biggles sprang to attention and bowed stiffly from the waist. 'Major Bigglesworth, your Highness, at your service,' he said crisply. 'Permit me.' He pulled out a chair from under the table.

The princess sat down, and, resting her arm on the table, regarded Biggles earnestly for some seconds. Then,

'Please forgive me for the manner in which I have intruded on your privacy,' she murmured. 'There were ... reasons ... you understand?'

'Yes, your Highness.'

'Will you please sit down? And you, Anna, remain near the door.'

Biggles remained standing, but the old woman took up a position with her back against the door.

'Where are your friends?' asked the princess.

'They are resting, your Highness.'

'Then do not disturb them now, although I should like to speak to them before I go, to thank them, as I now thank you, for what you are doing for Maltovia. I came – I felt I had to come—' The princess broke off, seeming to be at a loss to know how to continue.

'You came to give me some orders, perhaps?' suggested Biggles, trying to help her.

'Some advice, rather. My conscience compels me to warn you that you are in – danger – here.'

'I have already gathered that, your Highness. I came prepared for it. Count Stanhauser told me as much before I left England.'

'He doesn't know all, for there are some things that I dare not put in writing. Also, matters have moved swiftly during the last twenty-four hours. The situation is worse, much worse.'

'May I ask the reason, your Highness?'

'The death of General von Nerthold has tended to bring matters to a head.'

'Ah, I feared as much.'

'He was one of the men whom I knew I could trust implicitly, one of whom I was sure – you understand?'

'Which implies that there are others of whom you are not sure?'

The princess looked a little taken aback by Biggles's blunt rejoinder. 'Er ... yes.'

'Forgive me if I appear presumptuous, your Highness, but my desire is to serve you. Would it be too much to ask you to name, for my guidance, those of whom you are not sure?'

The princess hesitated. 'Perhaps that would not be quite fair,' she said slowly. 'I might do some one an injustice.'

'You have no positive proof of – disloyalty?'

'No.'

'But you suspect?'

'Yes.'

'General Bethstein?'

The princess started and caught her breath. What little colour there was in her face drained away, and she glanced around apprehensively. 'Ssh!' she breathed. 'It is dangerous to say such things. Walls have ears in Maltovia today.'

'Even so, your Highness, to speak plainly is a risk that surely must be taken, if Maltovia is to emerge triumphant from her troubles. It would be even more dangerous to remain silent.' Biggles moved forward impulsively, his heart touched by something in the girl's face, for she was no more than a girl. 'Your Highness, you came here to tell me something,' he continued in a low voice. 'I implore you to tell me what it is, or who it is you fear, in order that I and the friends who have come to help you may serve you to the best of our ability. You must trust us, or all our efforts will be in vain.'

'Yes, I do trust you,' answered the princess simply. 'Will you tell me the reason why you think I have not complete confidence in the commander of my army?'

'Do such trivial details matter, your Highness? The

53

more important question is, is it true, for if it is, I can see no other ending to this affair than the subjugation of Maltovia. Come, your Highness, you stand to lose your throne, your people their homes, and we our lives. This is no time for doubt or indecision. Those whom you know you can trust must work in perfect accord. Was it not your fear of the general that brought you here, and led you to adopt this disguise, instead of receiving us officially at the palace?'

The princess faltered. It was obvious from her manner that she had hardly been prepared for Biggles's direct methods. His intense personality was drawing her secrets from her; or it may have been his sincerity that moved her to speak. 'I will tell you all I suspect,' she said, in a low voice. 'You see, with Count Stanhauser, General von Nerthold was my friend and adviser. I appointed him to the rank of commander-in-chief when General Bethstein hoped for the supreme command. The result of this was that General Bethstein gradually withdrew from my court. Then for a while he travelled abroad.'

'Not in Lovitzna, by any chance?'

'Ah, that is something I do not know. But he gathered about him his own party, as invariably happens in such cases. Still, while General von Nerthold was alive I felt quite safe. Now he has gone, I am alone. General Bethstein appointed himself commander-in-chief—'

'Your pardon, Highness. Did you say appointed *himself?*'

'That is what it amounted to. Possibly by promises of appointments he succeeded in procuring enough votes to get himself appointed.'

'And had you no say in the matter?'

'My powers are limited by constitutional law. I could have appealed to the people, but that might have split the country into two halves at a time when it must stand united, or fall.'

'And General Bethstein is responsible for the national defences?'

'Yes.'

'What would happen if Lovitzna seized Maltovia?'

'I should be deposed.'

'And General Bethstein, if he made the conquest easy for the enemy, might step into your shoes under the protection of the Lovitznian government.'

The princess's eyes dilated in her agitation. 'Hush!' she breathed.

'In England,' went on Biggles, almost ruthlessly, 'we have a saying, "Call a spade a spade." General Bethstein has already profited by the death of General von Nerthold in that he has taken his place. Is he ambitious?'

'Yes. It was chiefly on that account that I withheld his appointment to commander-in-chief. That, and the fact that I did not trust him.'

'So it would seem that the time is ripe for him to further his ambitions.'

The princess's lips formed the word, 'Yes.'

'And that is why you fear him, why you came here in disguise, to see whether we were your friends – or his?'

'Yes.'

Biggles rose. 'Thank you, your Highness. I fear I have been persistent, but what you have told me merely confirms a half-formed suspicion in my own mind. Ludwig Stanhauser is to be trusted, I think?'

'Yes – yes. I trust him as myself.' The princess was emphatic.

'Possibly he was attached to us on your orders?'

'Yes, he was. I have been in communication with his uncle.'

'Thank you again, your Highness. You have clarified the position considerably. The existence of two parties in the country, yours and General Bethstein's, is going to make things rather complicated, I fear; but by working together, the outcome may not be that which General Bethstein desires. We shall see.'

The princess rose. 'I must go,' she said quietly. 'I did not intend to tell you all this; I really came to warn you and thank you for what you did this morning. I have heard about the battle with the Lovitznian aeroplanes.'

'That was a very small thing, your Highness. If we encounter no greater difficulties than that our task will not be a severe one.'

The princess started back as the handle of the door rattled sharply. 'Hey! Wake up and open the door,' came Algy's voice, cheerfully. 'What's the idea? It's nearly dinner time.'

Biggles walked quickly to the door, opened it, and locked it again as soon as Algy and Ginger were inside. They stopped dead, staring, when their eyes fell on the princess.

'Your Highness,' said Biggles before they could speak, 'may I present Lieutenants Lacey and Hebblethwaite?' He caught Algy's eye. 'Her Royal Highness, the Princess Mariana of Maltovia.'

Algy and Ginger, their eyes still wide with astonishment, sprang to attention. And while they were still standing thus, the silence was broken by a loud voice in the corridor. There was no mistaking the speaker. It was General Bethstein.

Chapter 7

On Thin Ice

Biggles thought the Princess was going to faint, but she recovered herself with an effort as he sprang to her side. 'Fear nothing,' he whispered. Then, more loudly, 'Don't speak – anybody.'

Came heavy footsteps in the corridor and, an instant later, the rattle of accoutrements, followed by a crash on the door as if it had been struck with a heavy object such as the hilt of a sword.

'Major Bigglesworth! General Bethstein to see you!' called a strange voice.

'Then give the general my compliments and tell him that I am not quite ready to receive visitors,' replied Biggles evenly. 'If he will go down and wait in the dining-room I will join him in a few minutes.'

There was a muttered conversation outside the door; then the general himself spoke. 'What I have to say cannot be said in a public room,' he announced harshly.

'Then be kind enough to wait in the next room while I get some clothes on,' returned Biggles cheerfully. 'I will send Lieutenant Lacey to entertain you.' As he spoke he beckoned to the princess and her woman-in-waiting and escorted them to a corner of the room where they could not be seen from the corridor when the door was opened. Then, to Algy, 'Go and hold him in conversation until I come,' he breathed.

Algy went quietly to the door, opened it and slipped

out. Biggles closed it quickly and leaned against it as voices receded down the corridor. The door of the next room banged. He took a peep outside and then addressed the princess. 'Come, your Highness, the coast is clear.'

'Thank you.' The princess held out her hand and Biggles kissed it gracefully.

'Before you go, tell me how I can get into touch with you should it be necessary,' he said.

'Ludwig Stanhauser will tell you,' she answered softly, and with that she was gone, closely followed by her maid.

Biggles walked to the end of the corridor, gave them a minute's grace, and then made his way to Algy's room.

'Things seem to be moving,' murmured Ginger, who was with him.

'They're moving a bit too fast,' answered Biggles with a worried frown. 'I had hoped to learn how to find my way about before this sort of thing started. However, ...' He opened the door of Algy's room and went in. 'Good evening, sir,' he greeted the general, who was standing back to the fireplace with two aides-de-camp, one a dark, sallow-faced man with Muscovite features, and the other a hard-faced youth with pale grey eyes, and a cruel thin-lipped mouth. 'Sorry I had to keep you waiting, but I did not anticipate this honour,' added Biggles. 'Shall we remain here, or would you rather go to my room?'

'We will go to your room,' replied the general, and without waiting for any further invitation he led the way. Biggles tried to reach the door first, but either by accident or design the general frustrated him, so he could only follow at his heels.

A few paces inside the room and the general stopped, sniffing. His eyes flashed to Biggles. 'Do I smell perfume?' he asked in a curious voice.

'My bath salts, I suppose,' returned Biggles lightly. 'It's a special brand I get in Paris.'

'You are fond of nice-smelling things – ha? Flowers, for instance.'

Biggles cursed inwardly as he followed the general's eyes and saw the basket of flowers still standing where Anna had placed it, but nothing of what he felt showed in his face. 'Yes, they're very nice, aren't they?' he returned blandly. 'I acquired them from an old woman. No doubt she thought they'd bring me luck. As a stranger, one likes to make a good impression, you know, and we airmen have a reputation for being superstitious.'

'So she told you they would bring you luck?'

'That's right.'

'I didn't know you spoke our language,' flashed back the general.

'Fortunately the old woman happened to speak a bit of German, of which I, too, know a little.'

'Ah, I understand.'

'Sit down, sir.'

'Lock the door, Menkhoff,' ordered the general, and the sallow-faced officer obeyed. 'Sit down, everybody.'

Biggles sat down in the chair just vacated by the princess, Algy and Ginger finding seats close to him.

'Now what I am going to say to you Englishmen is in confidence,' continued the general.

'Of course,' murmured Biggles smoothly.

'And I must be brief, for I have much to do. Therefore we will not – how do you say? – mince matters.'

'That should save time.'

'First of all, I will say that your presence here causes me profound anxiety.'

'On what account?'

'It is highly dangerous.'

59

'We are accustomed to danger.'

'You fail to understand me. I want no trouble with the British. If your government learn that you are here it might be bad for Maltovia.'

'From what I can see of things, it would be worse for Maltovia if we were not here,' returned Biggles imperturbably.

'Suppose you were killed; what should we tell the British Foreign Office?'

'Why tell them anything?'

'They would demand an explanation.'

'They already have it. Before leaving England I deposited a document at my bank. In the event of anything happening to us the manager will forward it to the Foreign Secretary. It is a full explanation and completely exonerates Maltovia.'

'I see,' muttered the general irritably, and set off on a new tack. 'Very well. Since you prefer to stay, you will, of course, come strictly under my orders.'

'Ah, there you are mistaken, general. I fear you must have been misinformed.'

'So?'

'Yes, that is so. My contract with Count Stanhauser appoints me to the sole command of the Maltovian Air Force, which is to be a separate service from the army.'

'That is wrong – entirely wrong.'

'The appointment was countersigned by Princess Mariana. 'You would not say that – she was wrong, I think?'

The general's lips tightened. Then he smiled, a cunning, ingratiating smile that did not deceive any one, least of all Biggles. 'If you will think the matter over, you will, I feel sure, perceive that it would be better for both of us if we worked in complete harmony,' he said suavely.

Now Biggles did not want to press the general too far; it

60

was too early for open enmity. Therefore he temporized. 'Of course,' he said quietly. 'It would be *much* better if we saw eye to eye with each other.'

'Then you will take your orders from me.'

'No, general, because I do not think that would be altogether advantageous. You see, you are not an airman. You know – correct me if I am wrong – little of air tactics. Speed is everything. If I had to wait for your orders an opportunity might be lost.'

'What are your immediate plans, then?'

'Tomorrow morning at dawn I shall lead our three machines on a patrol in the north-east corner of the principality, along the Lovitznian frontier, on a flight of reconnaissance. Naturally we are anxious to get our landmarks* fixed.'

'Yes, I think that would be a good thing to do. And after that?'

'It is a little too early to say. Would it not be better to wait to see what transpires? It is quite likely that I shall take the camera in order to get some photographs of the advanced Lovitznian positions. You could do with them, I imagine?'

'Yes, I could,' agreed the general, in an odd tone of voice.

Biggles stood up. 'Then that's settled,' he said cheerfully. 'I am glad that we shall be working together. It was nice of you to come and call on us.'

The general rose slowly to his feet. 'We must dine together sometime,' he said, without enthusiasm.

'Why not tonight?'

---

* As pilots new to the area, Biggles and his friends need to learn to recognize the important features of the landscape such as rivers and railway lines to help them navigate.

'No, I have other engagements.'

Biggles saw the general to the door. 'Do not hesitate to let me know if we can be of service to you at any time,' he said.

'I will let you know,' replied the general. Then, rather abruptly, 'Good night.'

'Good night, sir.'

Biggles waited until the footsteps of the general and his staff had died away. Then, after a surreptitious peep along the corridor, he closed the door and locked it.

'I wouldn't have told that old scab what we were going to do tomorrow morning, had I been you,' declared Algy wrathfully.

Biggles looked up. 'What gave you the idea that I did?'

'I heard you tell him that we were going to patrol the north-east corner—'

Biggles waved him to silence with a quick movement of his hand. 'That's only what I *told* him, you silly ass,' he said quietly. 'You don't suppose for a moment that we're going that way, do you?'

'Then where are you going?'

'I'm going where I trust we shall be able to shoot up a Lovitznian two-seater, and that won't be in the north-east corner of Maltovia.'

'Where will it be then?'

'Right over the aerodrome, I hope. With us out of the way – as they will fondly imagine, if I have got our precious general correctly weighed up – the enemy will send a machine over with the laudable idea of having a look at our aerodrome, which Bethstein has done his best to make conspicuous by providing us with a hangar that can be seen from one end of the country to the other.'

Algy's jaw dropped. 'Great Scott!' he muttered. 'I'm beginning to see which way the wind is blowing.'

'You'll feel which way it's blowing, too, before you're much older, I fancy. Come on. We've got a busy evening in front of us.'

'Where are you going?'

'First of all, we'd better have a bite of dinner. I want a word or two with Ludwig before I go to bed, and I also want to see Smyth and Carter. We ought to have a look at the machines to make sure they are ready for the morning. I hope to be in the air by dawn; with luck, we shall be able to give Ginger a little instruction in the gentle art of two-seater strafing*. Let's be going.'

* Air combat tactics, attempting to shoot down or force down an enemy aircraft.

Chapter 8

First Blood

After a quick dinner they set off at a brisk walk towards the aerodrome, which, owing to the flat nature of the country, was less than a mile from the outskirts of the town. On account of the lateness of the hour – it was nearly nine o'clock – Biggles had decided to speak to Smyth first.

'We ought to have asked Josef to call us at five,' declared Biggles as they walked. 'But I had no idea I should sleep so long. Smyth will be wondering what on earth we've been doing.'

'Will he have shifted the stuff across to the wood yet, do you think?' asked Algy.

'I doubt it, although it would depend on how many men Ludwig sent. If they got a way cleared through the trees it wouldn't take them long to put up a rough lean-to, which will serve while something more substantial is being built. Smyth is no fool; he saw the folly of leaving the machines and all our stores in that eyesore of a hangar. Still, we'd better go to the hangar first, in case he's there.'

'I think we could take a short cut across here,' suggested Ginger, pointing to a gap in the hedge, for the road they were on ran along the boundary of the aerodrome.

'Yes, you're quite right, it will cut off a big corner,' agreed Biggles, as he pushed his way through the gap and set off towards the hangar, the outline of which could now be seen against the starlit sky.

Nothing more was said, and it was no doubt due to their silence that an incident occurred which was to have a far-reaching effect on their plans. They had nearly reached the hangar, which they now saw was in darkness, when a figure, little more than a fleeting shadow, crossed the short stretch of turf that separated the hangar from the road. There was something so furtive about it that Biggles stopped at once, catching the others by the arms. Not a word was spoken. Then, as there came a soft rasping sound from out of the darkness, Biggles began to move forward, slowly, taking care not to brush his feet against the grass. Again he stopped, not more than ten yards away, his eyes trying to pierce the gloom, from which came a gurgling sound, as of liquid being poured. The sound stopped abruptly and, moving slowly forward, the airmen could just see a figure bending down near the wall of the hangar. Suddenly it began to back away, and a match flared up, revealing the man's silhouette. The light shone on the white fabric, and on something else, something that lay where it had been dropped near the canvas wall. Unmistakably it was a petrol can.

Biggles, understanding, sprang forward; but he was too late. The man flicked the match, and a sheet of flame leapt across the grass to the hangar.

At the sound of someone approaching, the man whirled round and saw the three airmen bearing down on him. His hand flew to his pocket and jerked up. 'Look out!' yelled Biggles, and flung himself aside just in time. A revolver roared. Three shots the man fired before he turned and fled towards the road. Whether it was due to his haste or the uncertain light is immaterial, but his aim was wild and the shots went wide. At the first, Biggles had whipped out his automatic, but he wavered in a turmoil of indecision, torn between anxiety for the machines which might be in

65

the hangar, and disinclination to allow the fire-raiser to escape. But when, as the flames swiftly consumed the fabric, he could see that the hanger was empty, he hesitated no longer, but raced after the man who had done the damage. He had by this time reached the road, where the flames reflected redly on the windscreen of a car.

The fugitive probably realized that he could not hope to open the door of the car, get inside, start the engine, and get clear before Biggles and his friends arrived. Anyway, with his foot on the running-board, he turned, and again threw up his revolver. Biggles was half-way through the hedge, in no position either to take cover or use his own weapon, but Algy saw his predicament and fired. The man twitched convulsively and collapsed in a crumpled heap beside the car.

'Now you've done it,' gasped Biggles, for they were all panting with exertion and excitement. 'You've killed him! You got him through the head. You—' The words died away on his lips as he stared aghast at the face of the fallen man. 'It's – it's – ' He seemed to find it difficult to speak.

'It's the general's staff-officer, the man he called Menkhoff,' muttered Algy, moistening his lips.

Biggles pulled himself together. 'Quick!' he snapped. 'Into the car with him.'

Ginger flung open the rear door of the car and the dead man was bundled inside. Biggles tossed his revolver in after him. 'Get in – get in,' he told Algy frantically. 'Get the car out of the way. There'll be a crowd here presently.'

'But where shall I take it?'

'Anywhere you like, but get it out of the way. Drive down the road until you come to a quiet spot, then leave it. Get back here as fast as you can, but keep inside the hedge so that you are not seen.'

Algy fell into the driving seat and grabbed the wheel with trembling hands. The car shot forward with a crash of gears and raced down the road.

Biggles looked at Ginger and shook his head. 'We're in a nice mess now,' he muttered. 'If Bethstein discovers that it was us who killed Menkhoff he'll have us shot.'

'Will he suspect us?'

'Possibly, but suspicion isn't proof. We shall have to swear that we know absolutely nothing about it. I hate all this lying, but when one is dealing with liars, one can't afford to tell the truth: it seems, not in war-time, anyway. Thank God, here comes Smyth.' They scrambled back through the hedge to meet Smyth and Carter who now came running up. 'Quick, Smyth,' cried Biggles anxiously. 'Tell me, did you get everything out of the hangar?'

'Everything, sir. It's under tarpaulins, amongst the trees.'

Biggles wiped his forehead with his sleeve. 'Thank heaven for that.'

'How did this happen, sir?' asked Smyth.

'This is how we found the hangar when we got to it,' replied Biggles, truthfully enough. 'We were on our way to see you. Listen, Smyth, there's going to be a first-class row about this, and we've got to clear ourselves from suspicion.'

'Of course, sir.'

'All right; then to prevent any argument I want you to say, if necessary, that we've been over by the machines with you for the last half-hour. We were all there together when we saw the hangar on fire and ran across to it. Is that clear?'

'As clear as a bell, sir.'

'You understand that, Carter?'

'Certainly, sir.'

'Good! Then don't depart from that story as you value your lives. Are the machines all right?'

'Right as rain. There was a hole or two in the fabric but we've patched them.'

'Have you filled the tanks? We want to get off before dawn.'

'Everything's ready, sir.'

'Good work, Smyth. I don't know what I should do without you. Have you both got revolvers?'

'Yes, sir.'

'Then get back to the machines and stand by. Don't allow any one to come near them under any consideration whatever. I'll tell you why as soon as I get a chance. All I can tell you now is that this place is rotten with spies and that they're likely to damage the machines. Look at this hangar if you have any doubt about that. It was the machines they were after. My word! they didn't waste any time. On second thoughts, I think you'd better wait here for a bit, Smyth. Carter, you get back now. Hello, who's this? Whoever it is, there won't be much to see but ashes.'

A car came racing down the road. It pulled up with a screech of brakes. A door slammed and presently a figure came running towards them. In the glow of the fast diminishing fire it was possible to make out the slim figure of Ludwig Stanhauser.

'What's happened?' he cried in a voice of anguish.

'The hangar caught fire,' Biggles told him simply.

'And the machines—?'

'Oh, they're safe enough.'

'Do you mean they weren't inside?'

'They were moved this afternoon. I didn't like this hangar: it was too conspicuous.'

'So you burnt it?'

'Good gracious, no! We were down here to make sure that our machines were in readiness for the morning when we saw the flames.'

'It's a relief to know they're all right,' answered Ludwig thankfully. 'I was at the palace talking to her Highness when we saw the glare from the window. I rushed down at once to see what had happened.'

'Then you can rush back and tell her Highness that all is well. Actually, the hangar is better out of the way. Anyhow, no harm has been done, that's the chief thing.'

'What are you going to do?'

'I'm going home to bed shortly, but I want a few words with you – urgently. Not here, though.'

'About something you've heard recently?' asked Ludwig in a low voice, at the same time throwing Biggles a knowing glance. 'Don't worry; I have heard about your visitor.'

'So she told you, eh?'

'Yes.'

'Good! We begin to understand each other, I think. We've got to work together, Ludwig. Can you come to my room tonight?'

'At what time?'

'Eleven o'clock.'

'I will be there.'

'Don't be seen. We must work in the dark – you understand?'

'I understand.' Ludwig looked around. 'By the way, where is Lacey?'

'He's some things to attend to. We didn't like to leave them without a guard,' answered Biggles vaguely, turning to Smyth. 'You get back now and relieve Mr Lacey,' he said.

'Very good, sir.' The NCO* saluted and marched away.

A small crowd had collected on the road, but it did not remain long. There were a few groans when it was seen what had happened, but the fire being nearly out, the people began to disperse. Algy appeared, rather breathless, as Ludwig moved towards his car. 'Eleven o'clock,' he whispered.

Biggles nodded.

'Can I give you a lift to the city?'

'No, thanks. I don't think it would be wise to be seen with you too much.'

'You may be right. I will see you later.'

Biggles turned to Algy as soon as Ludwig was out of earshot. 'Where did you put the car?' he asked quietly.

'About a mile down the road, as you suggested. I came to an overgrown drive, and shoved it in there.'

'Fine. You didn't leave any personal property in the car, I hope.'

'No fear. And I wiped the wheel with my handkerchief to remove any fingerprints.'

'Wise man,' declared Biggles.

'What's the next move?'

'I don't think there is any point in staying here any longer. The fire is out; Smyth and Carter are on guard. I think we might as well go home.'

As the three airmen reached the road, which by this time was nearly deserted, a big car came racing along heading for the city. They stood back to let it pass, and as it flashed by Biggles clutched Algy's arm.

'You saw who that was?'

'Bethstein,' answered Algy. 'By thunder, didn't he look savage!'

* Non-commissioned officer i.e. a Corporal or a Sergeant.

'Yes,' agreed Biggles, 'he certainly did. That's nothing to how he'll look when he learns what has happened to his friend.'

A quarter of an hour's sharp walk brought them to the hotel. Josef met them in the vestibule. He was very excited. 'There vos peen murder!' he said in a hoarse voice.

'Oh, and who has been killed?' asked Biggles calmly.

'Der Colonel Menkhoff.'

'Really! Where did it happen?'

'Right by der general's 'ouse.'

Biggles was about to pass on, but he pulled up short. '*Where* did you say?'

'In der drive of der General Bethstein's garten. Colonel Menkhoff – shot froo der brains.'

'And where is General Bethstein's house?'

'Down der road, just past der new aerodrome.'

Biggles shook his head sadly. 'Poor fellow,' he said solemnly.

But once they were behind the closed door of his room he sank down in a chair and eyed Algy meditatively. 'With the whole of Maltovia at your disposal, you would go and chose Bethstein's own drive to park that confounded car in, wouldn't you?' he sneered sarcastically.

'How the dickens was I to know it was his?' cried Algy helplessly.

'No, I suppose you weren't to know,' agreed Biggles. Then a smile broke over his face. 'Maybe it's all for the best,' he said optimistically. 'It will certainly give the general something to think about. Ring the bell for Josef. I could do with a drop of something hot. For our first day here we seem to have been what you might call busy.'

Chapter 9

Biggles Makes Some Suggestions

Punctually at eleven o'clock Ludwig arrived. He came unannounced. A gentle tap on the door; it opened and he walked in, in mufti, with his hat pulled well down over his eyes, and the fur collar of his heavy coat turned up so that he was almost unrecognizable.

'Come in, Ludwig,' said Biggles quietly. 'Algy, lock the door.'

Ludwig advanced into the room.

'The weather is turning colder, I see,' continued Biggles, smiling, as he helped Ludwig off with his coat.

'The weather may be getting colder but some things are getting hotter, I can tell you,' declared Ludwig.

Biggles laughed. He perceived that the lad had a sense of humour.

'Have you heard about the death of Colonel Menkhoff?' asked Ludwig breathlessly.

'Yes, we've heard about it.'

'A nice time for a thing like that to happen; it has started a rare old crop of rumours. Bethstein is raving like a madman.'

'That needn't worry us, need it?' inquired Biggles gently.

Ludwig threw him a curious glance as he sat down. 'I don't know,' he said slowly. 'Bethstein is a dangerous man.'

'So are we all – all dangerous men, if it comes to that.'

'You may be right, but I am afraid of Bethstein.'

'Come, come, Ludwig, that's a sad confession. It won't do to be afraid of him – or any one else – at this juncture.'

'You don't know Bethstein as well as I do,' returned Ludwig a trifle bitterly.

Biggles's easy manner underwent a swift change. His body stiffened and his expression became grim. 'Listen, Ludwig,' he said tersely; 'this funk* complex of yours where Bethstein is concerned has got to be kept under control. You say things are serious. Do not suppose for one moment that I am unaware of it. Very well. My answer to that is that this dilly-dallying has got to stop; if we are going to be of any use here we've all got to act, and act firmly, ruthlessly if necessary, regardless of whose toes we tread on. Aviation in the real sense of the word is only a side issue. I did not come here prepared to mess about with your internal organization or politics, but while things go on as they are now, with enemies working against us here in Janovica, anything we do in the air is likely to be so much wasted effort. Well, I've no time to waste; life is too short.'

'By heavens! don't think that I do not realize that,' answered Ludwig distractedly. 'What do you suggest? Is there anything we can do?'

'There are a lot of things we've *got* to do, or we might as well pack up right now.'

'Tell me one.'

'We've got to have a good spring-clean at home before we start looking elsewhere.'

'What do you mean by that?'

* slang: fear.

'What I say. We've got to put things on the ground into such shape that our actions in clearing the air overhead are likely to be seen in true perspective, not only by the people of this country but by other nations who will be watching, and that cannot be done by half-hearted measures.'

'Too well I know it. The question is, what to do first?'

'We've got to get Bethstein out of the way, for a start.'

Ludwig stared. 'Are you mad?' he gasped.

'Mad or not, we've got to do it. The man is a bigger danger than the Lovitznian army. Tell me, has he a big following behind him?'

'He has a number of officers with him, but the men dislike him.'

'Good! Who are these officers who are with him?'

'Most of them are foreigners brought into the country by him to help to reorganize the army on modern lines – at least, that was the excuse he gave for bringing them in.'

'Mercenaries, eh? Well, you'll see how they'll behave when we show them which side their bread is buttered. Who is the big noise behind Bethstein?'

'Klein.'

'Klein – who's he?'

'He's a banker; to be precise, the president of the Maltovian National Bank.'

'Is he a Maltovian?'

'No.'

'What nationality is he?'

'I don't know; I don't think anybody knows. He calls himself a cosmopolitan; actually he is, I imagine, an international financier.'

Biggles pursed his lips. 'How the dickens did such a state of affairs come about?'

'We got into monetary difficulties some time ago and Klein came forward and helped us out.'

'With an eye on the future, no doubt.'

'We know that now; we guessed it as soon as we saw that he had control of our finances. But we didn't know it then. We were glad of any assistance.'

'Whom do you mean by "we"?'

'The princess, my uncle, myself, and one or two others who think on the same lines as we do.'

'What might be called the all-Maltovian party?'

'That's what it amounts to.'

'Well, you seem to have got yourselves into a nice mess one way or another. Why in the name of heaven did your uncle who, as far as I can see, should be the princess's right-hand man, go to London?'

'The princess sent him.'

'Why?'

'Because two attempts were made on his life here, and she feared for him.'

Biggles grimaced. 'That's pretty grim,' he confessed. 'Your enemies are not worried by scruples, evidently. Neither, then, need we be. I have a short way of dealing with assassins. To come back to this fellow Klein. Who are the fellows who work in the bank?'

'They're Maltovians.'

'Thank goodness for that; it should make it easier to remove Mr Klein.'

'But that's madness; it's impossible.'

'I don't like that word, Ludwig. You, like a lot of other people, fall back on it too easily. Few things are impossible when you get down to brass tacks. You follow my advice and I'll show you whether or not it's impossible to get rid of your precious banker, if, as you say, he is working with Bethstein. You talk about it being madness to shift him; I say it would be madness to let him stay. If you do he'll wreck the ship, that's certain.'

Ludwig sprang suddenly to his feet. 'Bigglesworth,' he said passionately, 'you're right. We've needed a man like you. For months we've done our best, but we are no match for these unscrupulous plotters, and you know how it is when everything is at stake; one hesitates ... procrastinates, fearing to make a false move, hoping perhaps for a miracle, or a stroke of luck.'

'Now you're talking sense, Ludwig,' agreed Biggles approvingly. 'Lady Luck is an unreliable mistress. If you will maintain your present attitude, and persuade the princess to support it—'

'She'll support what I recommend,' broke in Ludwig confidently.

Biggles stared at him for a moment. 'I see,' he said slowly. 'So that's the way the wind blows, is it?'

A pink flush tinged Ludwig's cheeks. 'What do you mean?' he asked haltingly.

Biggles laid a hand on his shoulder. 'Listen, Ludwig,' he said softly. 'One of my bad habits is bluntness. I hate beating about the bush, as we say, maybe because I like to get my facts right, and keep my feet planted on solid ground. You're very fond of your princess, aren't you?'

Ludwig went scarlet. 'What if I am?' he demanded defiantly.

'Well, that's all right with me,' Biggles told him in a fatherly fashion. 'In fact, I'm glad to know it, because that puts you on the princess's side without any possible shadow of doubt, and at the same time tempers you for any risk, or even sacrifice, that may be demanded.'

'I'm prepared to die for the princess at any moment.' Ludwig spoke the words sincerely, without any suggestion of braggadocio.

'That's how I like to hear a man talk,' returned Biggles. 'Now then, let's get down to business. First of all, you can bet your life that Bethstein is doing some pretty hard thinking at this very minute.'

'You mean, because of Menkhoff being killed?'

'Yes.'

'I wonder who killed him?'

'You needn't wonder any longer. We did.'

Ludwig's face turned ashen and his jaw dropped. 'Good gracious!' he breathed. 'You had the nerve to murder him?'

Biggles shook his head. 'Oh, no, nothing like that,' he said quickly. 'On the contrary, he tried to murder us. We caught him red-handed at sabotage. It was he who fired the hangar, no doubt imagining that the machines were inside. When he saw that he was discovered he drew his revolver and fired three shots at us. Algy fired back in self-defence, and the shot hit him in the head and killed him. He was an enemy of Maltovia so I shan't lose any sleep on that account, and neither need you. I only wish it had been Bethstein himself. Well, now you know the facts; I've only told you this because we can't afford to have secrets from each other. One result of the affair may be that it will cause Bethstein to push forward his plans. We, therefore, shall have to do the same thing.'

'Yes, but what can we do?'

'As I have already said, we must clip Bethstein's wings. I realize that it might be difficult to take away his command without causing a serious row, so this is the way we shall have to curtail his activities. The princess must form a Ministry of Defence, with your uncle as president. He must come home; he is much too valuable to be left in England. The new ministry appointed, the general will have to take his instructions from it – that's how it's done in Great Britain, and if it is good enough for Great Britain it ought to be good enough for Maltovia. Needless to say, the ministry will consist only of men who are absolutely above suspicion. That should tie Bethstein's hands somewhat.'

'I never thought of that way,' declared Ludwig enthusiastically. 'It gives us supreme power without giving anyone cause for complaint. But suppose the general refuses to obey the ministry's orders?'

'That would be gross insubordination, and would provide us with the only excuse we need to get rid of him altogether.'

'Of course. Why, it's a marvellous idea,' asserted Ludwig, who was trembling with excitement. 'I'll speak to the princess immediately, and tell her to send for my uncle.'

'Fine! That's item number one, which brings us to number two. Now there is just a chance that when Bethstein gets wind of what is afoot he may take the bull by the horns and rush things. We've got to short-circuit his most likely move, which will be, obviously, to get the Lovitznian army on the march. Now I've studied the map pretty closely, particularly the north-east corner of Maltovia, which is the only direction from which the Lovitznians could come. As I see it, the river Nieper forms a fine natural obstacle.'

'The Nieper is in Lovitzna.'

'I know, but only just, and it runs parallel with the frontier – so much so that I wonder it doesn't form the boundary.'

'It used to, years ago, before the Lovitznians collared that piece of territory.'

'No matter. The point is, to get here the Lovitznians

must cross that river, and as far as I can see there is only one bridge.'

'That is correct. It was built by the Lovitznian government not long ago.'

'No doubt for the purpose for which they now hope to use it.'

'Of course. Again, we realize that now, but at the time we thought it was a splendid thing because it opened a great highway for commerce between the two countries.'

'The old, old story. Well, it is across that bridge that the Lovitznian army must march. What is it built of – wood, steel, concrete or what?'

'Concrete. It's a double bridge. The railway goes underneath and the road runs above it.'

'That's excellent; concrete cracks very easily.'

'What do you mean?'

'That bridge is going up in a cloud of dust and pebbles.'

Ludwig stared aghast. 'That bridge cost nearly five million pounds to build. Lovitzna would throw a thousand fits.'

'Let 'em. They can tie themselves up in convulsions as far as we're concerned once the bridge is down.'

'They'll complain.'

'So will you. You will be most upset, and send them a note asking what the dickens they mean by destroying the bridge, pointing out that by severing commercial relations they are deliberately trying to cause trouble.'

'But they won't believe that.'

'Of course they won't; neither will any one else, but that doesn't matter. My dear boy, that is what is called diplomacy. Maltovia will sit with its tongue in its cheek while all the nations who dislike Lovitzna and her big ally will rock with laughter. Naturally, under the pretence of being alarmed, the princess will be justified in moving her most loyal regiments up to the frontier to watch her interests. At present, such a move would be regarded as a threat, almost an act of war, but the destruction of the bridge would provide a valid excuse.'

'My word! I wish you were Prime Minister of Maltovia,' muttered Ludwig admiringly.

'I haven't finished yet. We've still got Klein to deal with, and this is how I suggest we do it. When the bridge goes up the Maltovian government will at once show its friendly spirit by offering to help build a new one, an even better one. They will, at the same time, declare their intention of building a new high road to that corner of the state. This, of course, will need money, for which it will be necessary to raise a loan of, say, ten million pounds. You will go to Mr Klein and ask him to lend you that sum. When he says – as he certainly will – that there is nothing doing, you will express your regret and say that if he can't oblige you, you will have to find some one else who will. You will then put the loan forward to one of the big friendly powers. They, seeing what is in the wind, will find the cash, and once they've got money in the country they'll take jolly good care to send some one to keep an eye on it. Then Mr Klein, if he stays, will have to watch his p's and q's.'

Ludwig was pale with excitement. 'How are you going to blow up the bridge?' he asked breathlessly.

Biggles looked pained. 'Me? Lovitzna will do that.'

'Lovitzna? What ... how...?'

'You'll see,' nodded Biggles calmly. 'By the way, what has happened to the two machines we shot down this morning? Has Lovitzna said anything about them yet?'

'No, but I expect there will be a fine old row. The pilots who got back will say what happened. We shall get a stiff note from the Lovitznian government. Goodness knows how we shall answer it.'

'You've no need to worry on that score. The princess will not have to look for an excuse. All you need do when the note comes in is raise your eyebrows and say, "Indeed! If you will explain to us what Lovitznian aeroplanes were doing over Maltovia, then we will go into the matter and endeavour to find out who is to blame." That will give them something to chew their pens over. It should take them a long time to find a reasonable excuse for flying over Maltovia. Don't you see that they will be in a cleft stick? They daren't say that they ordered the machines to fly over Maltovia because that would be an act of war in flagrant violation of international law; to save their faces they can only say that their pilots must have lost their way, in which case you will simply tell them to blame their pilots, not us. You might send some troops out to the crashes to salve anything worth saving. One last thing. I want you to send some one you can trust, a motor-cyclist dispatch rider for preference, up into the north-east corner of the country. He will watch the sky and make a careful note of what he sees.'

'But he won't see anything. There is no flying up there.'

'There will be, I think, tomorrow morning.'

'What makes you think that?'

'A little bird has whispered in my ear.'

'What bird?'

Biggles smiled. 'Perhaps I had better explain. I told Bethstein that we should do a patrol up there at dawn to-morrow. If the air there is full of Lovitznian fighters trying to get us, it will prove – since we have told no one else – that Bethstein is in communication with the enemy. It will also serve other purposes. It will keep the Lovitznian fighters out of the way, and enable us – providing your man is smart enough to count them – to get an idea of the enemy's aerial strength.'

'And what are you going to do?'

'I shall be waiting over this city for the Lovitznian two-seater, which will, I hope – since we shall be assumed to be out of the way – take the opportunity of slipping across on a reconnaissance.'

'And you will shoot it down in flames?'

'Not if I can prevent it. I shall endeavour to persuade the pilot to land.'

'What will you do with him?'

'Hand him over to you to pop into a nice strong prison cell where he can be forgotten for the time being.'

'And the machine?'

'That's what I really want.'

'For what purpose?'

'To drop a bomb on the Nieper bridge. You see, if a Lovitznian aeroplane blows up a Lovitznian bridge, Lovitzna can't very well accuse Maltovia, can she?'

Ludwig stared at Biggles like a man in a dream. 'Yes,' he said, as though he was talking to himself, 'we needed some one like you on our side.'

Biggles smiled as he stood up. 'Well, Ludwig, that's my idea of the lines on which we should work. Now you run along and do your part. Not a word to a soul, except, of course, the princess. Get your uncle back as quickly as possible. We are going to get some sleep, for we look like having a busy day tomorrow. Goodnight.'

There was a new spring in Ludwig's stride as he left the room.

Chapter 10

Combat!

It was a bleak morning, with frosty stars twinkling in the sky and a raw wind blowing from the north, when, at five o'clock, the three airmen let themselves quietly out of the hotel and, with extra sweaters and their flying-kit over their arms, made their way to the aerodrome. Smyth and Carter were awaiting them, and to them Biggles announced himself satisfied with the arrangements they had made for the housing of the aircraft and stores. It was crude, but, with fir branches covering the roof of the shelter – it was no more than that – it would be practically impossible to see it from above. A lane, flanked by the trees that had been felled, gave access to the aerodrome itself.

After a glance round, Biggles declared his intention of taking off right away. 'I want to be at twenty thousand, possibly higher, by daybreak, so the more sweaters we can get on under our flying-kit, the better; we shall need them, if I know anything about it. Stand by, Smyth, until we get back.'

'Very good, sir.'

Biggles turned to Ginger. 'I want you to obey orders to the letter,' he said curtly. 'You know the scheme. We want to force a machine down intact if we can. If not – well, we'll shoot it down, anyway. But you keep out of it if you can. I can't say definitely that you are not to take part in anything that may transpire, because an exceptional opportunity might come your way, in which case it would be foolish not to take advantage of it. But your chief business is to watch; watch how Algy and I go to work if we attack anything; at the same time you must watch your own tail. We may, of course, draw blank; on the other hand, we might run into a two-seater with an escort of scouts; these chances are all on the boards, so watch your step. All right; if every one is ready we'll get off.'

The engines were started, and after they had been run up to make sure that they were giving their revs, the machines taxied down the lane to the open field. The sky was just beginning to turn grey in the east as the machines took off in formation with Biggles at the point of the V, and after circling the aerodrome once or twice he struck off on a north-easterly course, which, as it happened, took them over General Bethstein's house. At least, Biggles assumed it was the house, for there was only one, and its location and tree-girt drive agreed with Algy's description of it. As he approached, at a height of rather less than a thousand feet, he saw light pour from a window as if a curtain had been hurriedly dragged aside. 'Looking to see which way we're going, I'll bet,' he mused, as he began to climb for height.

Up, up, up, and ever upward he held the nose of his machine, still heading towards the north-east corner of the little state, noting landmarks all the way, and not until his altimeter registered twelve thousand feet did he make a wide turn and begin to fly back over his course. The sky turned grey, from grey slowly to lavender, and then to pale blue. In spite of the cold, it looked like being a fine day. At eighteen thousand feet, with Janovica looking like a collection of dolls' houses far to the south-west, he altered his course again, this time to north-east by east, to bring the formation into a position that would intercept anything approaching from the direction of Lovitzna. And still he climbed. At twenty thousand, however, he levelled out, and throttled back to the slowest cruising speed his machine could hold and yet maintain altitude.

Time and time again he pushed up his goggles and peered long and carefully round the end of his windscreen into the north-east, but from horizon to zenith the blue was unbroken. To and fro he led the formation, ever watching the north-east, with the city of Janovica always in sight in the far distance. Ten minutes passed; twenty, and there was still no sign of the enemy. He looked over his shoulder at Algy, sitting like a dummy some twenty yards behind and to the left of him. Algy caught his eye and pulled a long face. Biggles shrugged his shoulders and returned to his vigil. Once his heart missed a beat as his eye caught a movement far below, but it was only an eagle, and he watched it sail past bound for an unknown destination.

A few minutes later a tiny speck appeared against the blue, considerably lower than they were. Quickly he pushed up his goggles to make sure that it was not a spot of oil on a lens, but no, it was still there. Joyfully he shook his wings and changed direction, flying directly into the orb of the sun, but never for an instant taking his eye off the speck. Magically, it seemed, it grew in size until it became an aeroplane, and a minute or two later he saw that it was a big, three-engined machine. He noticed, too, that it held steadily on its way, flying a direct course that would, in about twenty minutes to half an hour, take it to Janovica. It drew level with the three single-seaters and then passed by, a good five thousand feet below and two miles to the west. Slowly, in order not to disturb the formation, Biggles turned, and then, putting down his nose, he tore down behind the stranger. In the usual curious way, it seemed to float up towards them, and a grim smile hovered about his lips as he picked out the brown crosses of Lovitzna.

He was now so close that he could see, through the crisp air, every detail of the big machine, which was of a type unknown to him, a tri-motored cantilever monoplane* with very tapered wings. The thing that amazed him at first was the careless behaviour – or else it was supreme self-confidence – of the one gunner, who, with his elbows resting on the side of his gun-mounting, and his chin cupped in the palms of his hands, was gazing down at the scenery with the casual disinterest of a railway traveller. Biggles then remembered that the Maltovian Air Force was supposed to be miles away, and assumed that this accounted for the gunner's calm assurance.

This attitude, however, was not to last much longer. Swiftly, with his guns aligned, Biggles drew nearer and nearer until he was not more than thirty feet behind, and just above the bomber, with the gunner still completely oblivious of his presence. Had his intention been the destruction of the machine the matter would have ended there and then, and the quite useless gunner might never have known whence came the shots that killed him. But Biggles had set himself a more difficult task. He wanted the machine intact, although whether or not he would succeed in this depended, he knew, upon the quality of the pilot. If he was a brave man, and he would need to be brave to face what was coming, he would fight to the bitter end, and the machine would inevitably crash. On the other hand, if he was a normal human being, with only an ordinary amount of courage, he would soon see that his hour had come, and make the best of a bad job by going down and landing at the first convenient place.

* three-engined aircraft – see cover illustration.

Biggles opened the proceedings by firing a short burst over the big machine, and his lips parted in a whimsical smile at the gunner's consternation. For perhaps three seconds he stared up white-faced at the three machines sitting on his tail, then he threw up his hands and disappeared from sight. Biggles assumed that he had gone through to speak to the pilot, and in this he soon saw that he was correct, for, by diving slightly, he could see the two Lovitznian airmen together in the glass-enclosed cockpit. Seeing that they were both looking at him, he leaned out as far as he could and jerked downwards with his gloved hand. The order was obvious, but it did not, however, suit the pilot of the big machine, for he immediately began to turn away; but he straightened out again with alacrity when Algy raced up on that side of him and fired a short burst across his nose.

The big machine was now flying straight again on its original course, almost hemmed in by the three fighters, and in that position it continued while several minutes passed. Again Biggles saw the pilot staring at him, and again he jabbed downwards, but as the other ignored the commands his patience gave out. Bringing his nose round, and praying that he would not hit anything vital, he deliberately fired a few shots into the machine. That they took effect was clear, for the pilot at once cut out his engine and began gliding down. Biggles followed, still pointing sternly downwards, and when he got a nod from the man in the pilot's seat of the big machine, he knew that he had won. 'If, after that, you try any funny tricks, my lad, you're for the high jump,' he muttered savagely to himself.

Glancing down, he saw to his surprise that they had almost reached Janovica, for in the excitement of the chase he had forgotten all about the city. Turning in his seat, he beckoned Ginger to come closer, and pointed to the

aerodrome, an indication that he – Ginger – was to lead
the way in; then, looking back at the enemy pilot, he made
him understand that he was to follow, which he did, as
meekly as a lamb. Biggles did not blame him for that; he
would have been a fool to do otherwise. If any blame
attached to any one it was to the gunner, who had so
unpardonably been caught off his guard, and thus let his
pilot down.

Ginger landed first, to be followed in close order by the
Lovitznian machine, and then the other two fighters.
Biggles taxied tail up to the foreigner and waited for the
pilot to alight before he switched off, then jumped down
and ran towards him. The two Lovitznians raised their
hands in token of surrender.

'Do you speak English?' asked Biggles, curtly.

The men shook their heads; it was obvious that they did
not.

Biggles pointed to the lane through the trees. 'March!'
he said. There could be no mistake about his meaning,
and the little party, encumbered in heavy flying-kit,
moved slowly towards the wood. In addition to normal
kit, the two Lovitznians were also equipped with parachutes, which considerably retarded their movements.

Biggles was wondering what he should do with his
prisoners when he saw a car racing down the road, and
was relieved when Ludwig jumped out and ran towards
them.

'You've got them!' he cried excitedly.

Biggles laid a finger on his lips, and handed over the
prisoners to Algy before turning to speak. 'Look here,
Ludwig,' he said earnestly, 'you've got to take charge of
these fellows, and there must be no mistake. On no
account must they be allowed to escape or the fat will be in
the fire. Can you fix things up?'

'Certainly. I have made the necessary arrangements in case you brought it off.'

'What are you going to do with them?'

'Take them to a special quarter in the state prison.'

'Can you do that without any one knowing about it?'

'I think so. The governor is a friend of mine.'

'Then see what you can do. I don't want Bethstein to know they are here or he will want to interview them and I don't want that to happen.'

'I'll take them along in my car. Not a word shall be said.'

'You realize that nothing must appear in the papers?'

'Leave that to me.' Ludwig had become a different man since the previous evening.

'All right, off you go.'

'I want to talk to you.'

'I haven't time now.'

'I have told the princess what you said, and my uncle is on the way home already, by air. We telephoned him.'

'Good! We can talk about it tonight.'

'At what time?'

'Six o'clock.'

'That will suit me very well. I will call for you at six. Some one wishes to speak to you.'

Biggles threw Ludwig a sidelong glance. 'I understand,' he said shortly. 'I'd like to have a word with you now, but you know what I hope to do; moreover, I don't want any one to see these two fellows. We'll go into things at six o'clock.'

'Very well, I'll get along.'

Biggles waited until the prisoners were on their way to prison in Ludwig's car, with his orderly sitting behind them on guard. Then he turned to Smyth. 'Is the big machine fitted with bomb racks?' he asked.

'Yes, sir.'

'Good! I hoped it would be. Sling on the two biggest you've got.'

'They're one hundred kilogrammes.'

'They'll do. Get them on as quickly as you can, and get Carter to look the machine over to find out where those shots of mine went. Don't trouble about them, though, unless they did any real damage.'

'Very good, sir.'

Biggles turned to Algy who was just coming out of the cabin door of the big machine. 'Anything interesting inside?' he asked.

'I'd say there is. Come and look at this.' Algy pointed to a bale of leaflets standing on the floor of the cabin. The string had already been cut.

'What the deuce are they?'

'I can't read what it says on them because the language is, I suppose, Maltovian, but I reckon they're propaganda – the sort of stuff both sides dropped over the lines during the last War. They must have been going to drop them over the city.'

'Good job we stopped that. There's no telling what mischief they might have caused. Haul the whole lot into the shed and throw something over them. We'll attend to them when we get back. Anything else?'

'Only a map.'

'Let's have a look at it.'

While the mechanics were busy on the machine, Biggles examined the map. Several lines had been drawn on it, and in one place an area had been encircled with a fine red line. 'Hello – hello, what's all this, I wonder?' he muttered. 'Unless I'm mistaken this map is going to tell us a useful story. We'll spend a bit of time on it tonight and try to work out what these lines mean.' He folded the map and handed it to Smyth. 'Put that in your pocket and don't lose it,' he said. 'Remember to give it to me when I come back.'

'There are some people coming down the road,' announced Ginger.

'Then we'll get off before they arrive,' declared Biggles. 'I don't want too many people to see what's going on. I can't quite make up my mind what to do about this machine; my original idea was to dump it somewhere as soon as we had bombed the bridge, but I must say it seems a pity to do away with it. It might be useful. The trouble about an aeroplane is that you can't disguise it.'

'We could paint out the markings,' suggested Ginger.

'I could paint it red, or some other colour, all over,' put in Smyth.

'Unhappily, paint doesn't alter the shape of a machine,' murmured Biggles. 'Never mind; perhaps we could keep it hidden. I'll bring it back, anyway, so you get your paint ready, Smyth, and fix up some sort of cover to put it under. I had better speak to Ludwig about some trustworthy men to form a guard to keep prowlers out of the wood. That's all for the moment; we shall have more time to discuss these things when we get back. Let's get away. Algy, you man the rear gun.'

'What about me?' asked Ginger.

Biggles hesitated. 'I think you'd better stay here,' he said.

Ginger's face fell. 'That's a bit thick,' he muttered in tones of the deepest disappointment.

Biggles reflected for a moment or two. 'All right, you can come if you like; you had better sit next to me and help to watch the sky.'

Ginger gave a little whoop and climbed into his seat. Biggles followed, and spent a few seconds examining the instrument-board of the big machine; but everything was, as he expected, of standard international pattern, and presented no difficulty. The engines were still hot, so, the usual warming-up being unnecessary, the bomber was soon in position to take off.

Biggles looked at Ginger, one hand on the throttle. 'Well, here we go for the fireworks,' he said.

The engines roared and the machine sped across the aerodrome.

Chapter 11

The Bridge – and a Capture

For an hour Biggles flew steadily into the north-east over rough, hilly country, heading on a straight course for his objective. Actually, he struck the river a little way above the bridge, but he soon picked it out in the distance. Before turning towards it, however, he flew up and down inside the Lovitznian frontier, his keen eyes searching the terrain for movements of enemy troops and war material. It was not necessary to look very hard, for evidence of the coming conflict was apparent everywhere – camps, lorries on the roads, and working parties of men.

'If we hadn't come here, the Lovitznians would be inside Maltovia within a week,' he told Ginger moodily, as he stared down at the military preparations. 'Apparently it has not occurred to Lovitzna that anything might happen to their lovely bridge. Look at the hills on our side of the river; with the bridge out of the way a handful of determined men could prevent the Lovitznians from getting across. Well, let's go and give them something to think about.'

As he spoke, Biggles turned the machine and headed back towards the river, steering for the bridge, which lay like a white road across the water. In this way, to any one watching the machine, it would appear to be coming from the heart of Lovitzna, certainly not from Maltovia.

At a distance of about two miles he throttled back and

began a long glide, at the same time lining the machine up with the bridge. Every few moments he glanced around the sky, but not another machine was in sight, so it may have been the simplicity of his task that brought a faint smile to his face.

'What are you laughing at?' asked Ginger.

'I was just thinking how simple this is compared with the jobs we had to do in France,' answered Biggles.

'Suppose some one is just going over the bridge?'

'Then it looks like being his unlucky day. It would be just too bad, as the Americans say. Can you see any one watching us?'

'There are some people who look like soldiers at each end of the bridge; I can see their faces so they must be staring up.'

'They'll have something else to stare at presently,' announced Biggles, as he steepened his glide into a dive. Dispassionately, his right elbow resting on the side of the cockpit, he watched the bridge apparently coming to meet the machine. So unconcerned was he that he might have been going to land on his own aerodrome, but he did not relax his vigilance, and in spite of his casual manner he was flying very carefully, for he had only two bombs and he could not afford to miss. The needle of the altimeter crept slowly back until it was actually resting on zero, although his height might have been two hundred feet as he glided, slowly now, over the blockhouse on the northern side of the river. His hand felt for the bomb toggle and gripped it. Still he waited, the machine flying at not much more than stalling speed, his feet applying the slight pressure necessary on one side of the rudder-bar* or the

* A foot-operated bar which moves the rudder, usually mounted at the rear of an aircraft, to turn left or right.

other. Suddenly he jerked his hand back. The machine rocked. Simultaneously he jerked the throttle wide open, thrust the stick forward and banked away steeply.

Ginger heard the roar of the explosion above the noise of the engines; he felt the machine surge upwards like a lift under its pressure, but for a moment he could see nothing owing to the cloud of smoke that rose high in the air over the centre of the bridge. Then, as it cleared and the middle of the bridge became visible, a cry of triumph broke from his lips. The two centre arches had completely disappeared. 'You've got it!' he yelled exultantly.

'Yes,' agreed Biggles, 'and I fancy it will take longer to fill up that gap than it did to make it.' As he spoke, he turned the machine and cruised back up the river.

'Where the dickens are you going?' asked Ginger in alarm.

'I'm just going to have a look at the damage, that's all,' replied Biggles casually. 'I also want the fellows down there – who, by the way, seem to be excited over something – to see us. Yes, we've certainly made a hole,' he continued, looking down as they passed over the shattered arches. 'Seems a pity to spoil a nice bridge like that, but there it is. Well, I think we might be getting home; we'd better go this way. It might not be wise to allow ourselves to be seen roaring straight back to Maltovia.' He turned, this time to the left, which took the machine further into Lovitzna; shortly afterwards he turned left again and flew parallel with the river, still well inside Lovitznian territory. It was flat, open country, mostly grassland on which grazed occasional herds of cattle. For the rest, it appeared to be sparsely populated. 'I don't think there is much to see here,' he murmured after a while, and was about to turn on the homeward course when he stiffened suddenly. 'Hello, what's this coming?' he said tersely.

Ginger had seen nothing, but following the direction of Biggles's eyes, he saw an aircraft coming up towards them from out of the west. 'My goodness! You don't miss much,' he muttered.

'It doesn't do to miss anything at this game,' Biggles told him. 'Go and make sure Algy has seen him.'

Ginger crept through into the rear cockpit, but Algy had already seen the stranger, and was leaning idly against his gun watching him. Ginger returned to his seat. 'Algy is watching him,' he told Biggles.

'It looks like a two-seater,' observed Biggles, 'but I can't see any one in the rear cockpit, can you?'

'If there is any one in it he must be sitting on the floor,' returned Ginger emphatically.

By this time the machine was only a few hundred yards away, slightly above them and a little to the right, but it had turned slowly in their direction. 'By gosh! It's one of the new high-performance Fokker day-bombers,' ejaculated Biggles, who was watching the machine with knitted brows.

'It's carrying Lovitznian markings, anyway,' cried Ginger in alarm.

'So are we, so I don't think we've anything to worry about,' replied Biggles. 'By the look of it I should say that it's a brand new machine, too,' he went on in a low voice, as if he were talking to himself. 'Coming out of the west? It must be a new machine just being delivered to the Lovitznian Air Force. By James, we could do with that ourselves.'

Ginger stared. 'You're not thinking of trying to capture it by any chance, are you?' he asked, a trifle sarcastically.

'As a matter of fact, that's just what I was thinking of,' answered Biggles evenly.

'You don't want me to board it in mid-air, or anything like that, I hope?'

'Nothing so desperate, Ginger. I never make life harder than it is. Give the chap a wave.'

The pilot in the bomber, evidently noting that the machine was a Lovitznian, was already waving, and Biggles lost no time in opening the side window of his cockpit and waving back. Then he looked down and noted that there were half a dozen fields within easy reach, each large enough to land in. 'Jab downwards, Ginger,' he ordered. 'Try to make him understand that we've come to meet him and that we want him to land.'

'OK,' cried Ginger, suddenly understanding.

Biggles did not wait. He throttled back and began gliding towards a big field some distance to the right.

Algy's head popped into the cockpit. 'Are you crazy?' he shouted. 'We're over Lovitzna.'

'Go back to your gun,' Biggles told him shortly, and a minute or two later his wheels touched lightly on the green turf of enemy country. 'What's he doing, Ginger?' he asked sharply.

'He's circling,' answered Ginger tersely. 'I think he's going to follow us down.'

'Fine! Leave the talking to me.'

Biggles jumped out as soon as the machine had finished its run, and beckoned to the pilot of the bomber, who was still circling the field, evidently undecided what to do. But at Biggles's vigorous invitation he waited no longer, but glided down, his machine coming to a standstill about a hundred yards from the other. The pilot climbed down stiffly, which suggested that he had come a long way. Biggles noticed also that he wore a parachute.

'Hello!' he called cheerfully. Do you speak English?'

The other looked surprised. 'You are English?' he queried, with a strong foreign accent.

'Yes, we are instructors to the Lovitznian Air Force.'

'Goot! I am Wengel. I have brought a new machine for you.'

'We were expecting it,' returned Biggles easily. 'In fact, we were sent to meet you. My chief has given some special instructions about the delivery of the machine.'

'So!'

'Yes, there is a big crowd waiting to greet you at the aerodrome, and the chief wants to celebrate the occasion by presenting you with a decoration – the Purple Pigeon of Lovitzna.'

'Dat vos very kind of him.'

'Not in the least, but I haven't finished yet. No one in Lovitzna has yet seen a parachute-jump, so he thought that if you happened to be wearing one it would be a good opportunity to provide the public with a spectacle, at the same time putting them into a good mood to subscribe for another machine.'

The other looked doubtful. 'I like not jumping,' he protested.

'It may mean a big order for machines.'

'But I no can jump and leave my machine alone.'

'Of course not; that's why we've brought a big one, and a spare pilot, who will fly your machine while you ride with us. When we get over the aerodrome you will jump out, while we shall follow and land beside you. It should please the crowd.'

The other shrugged his shoulders. 'It is unusual,' he said, and in this Biggles was in mental agreement with him. 'Goot! Very well, so shall it be. Let us go now, for I am hungry.'

'There will be something waiting for you on the aerodrome,' Biggles told him warmly; and he meant it, although he was not thinking of food.

They had a few draws at cigarettes which the German delivery pilot produced, and then they took their seats, the German in the big machine and Algy in the light bomber. In a few minutes they were in the air, heading for the central airport of Lovitzna, which was also the chief Air Force station. Twenty minutes brought them to it, and Biggles turned to his passenger. 'Well, here we are,' he said lightly. 'Over you go.'

'I see no crowds,' muttered the German suspiciously.

'They are all inside the hangars to make sure that they don't get in the way,' declared Biggles. 'The Lovitznians are not like us, you know; they are apt to get excited, and the chief thought they might rush out and get hurt.'

The German nodded and climbed out on to the wing. 'I will see you presently,' he cried, and leapt into space.

A slow smile broke over Biggles's face as he watched the parachute open and the luckless German sail downward.

Ginger came through from the rear cockpit. He was shaking with laughter, but he tried to adopt a serious pose. 'I call that a bit steep,' he declared. 'What is he going to tell the people down there when he arrives without a machine?'

'I haven't the faintest idea,' replied Biggles. 'But whatever he tells them you can be pretty sure that it won't be received with cheers of joy. Well, well, all's fair in love and war, so they say. Where's Algy? – ah, there he is.'

Algy was cruising round the larger machine, and he took position behind it as Biggles turned for home.

'By gosh! Look what's coming!' cried Ginger.

Biggles leaned forward and peered through the windscreen. Half a dozen single-seaters were coming towards them from the direction of Maltovia, led by one that carried black pennants on its wing struts.

'Are they after us, do you think?' asked Ginger anxiously.

'No. They're just coming back from a patrol, I expect.'

And such, presumably, was the case, for the pilots of the Lovitznian squadron gave them a cheerful wave as they sailed past.

'Won't they be sick when they get home and discover what has happened – that they were within fifty yards of us without knowing who we were!' chuckled Ginger.

'I don't expect it will improve their tempers,' smiled Biggles. 'But let's get home ourselves before we laugh too loudly.'

'It will take us all our time to make the aerodrome before dark, won't it?'

'We ought to just about do it. As a matter of fact, that will suit us very well. Had it been broad daylight we should have been compelled to land somewhere else. I mean, the people in Maltovia might well wonder what is going on if they see two Lovitznian machines landing. I don't want any one to see us if we can prevent it.'

For this reason Biggles kept well to the western side of the state as they flew down it, for there the country was but thinly populated. When he drew level with Janovica, however, he turned to the east, and with the sun just sinking below the horizon he crept over the forest into the aerodrome. Landing, he taxied quickly up the runway between the trees, closely followed by Algy.

Smyth, a rifle in his hand, came running to meet them. 'What's this?' he cried to Biggles, at the same time pointing to Algy's machine.

'A little present from Lovitzna,' replied Biggles as he switched off.

Smyth nodded solemnly. 'We shall have quite a respectable air force presently, sir, if we go on collecting machines at this rate,' he grinned.

'Hello, this looks like Ludwig's car coming down the road,' put in Ginger. 'He's got his foot down, too, by the rate he's moving.'

The car skidded to a standstill and Ludwig ran towards them.

Biggles flicked the ash off the cigarette he had lighted. 'Something's happened,' he said quietly.

'What makes you think that?' asked Algy quickly.

'You have only to look at his face.'

Ludwig was pale as he ran up. His manner was agitated, almost distraught.

'What's the trouble, Ludwig?' asked Biggles curtly.

'The Count,' gasped Ludwig. 'You know he was flying here?'

'Crashed?'

'Worse, if anything,' declared Ludwig hoarsely. 'He's down in Lovitzna.'

Chapter 12

A Blow and a Desperate Mission

'How did it happen?' asked Biggles grimly, after a moment's silence broken only by Ludwig's deep breathing.

'He got into the wrong machine at Belgrade.'

'By accident?'

'I don't think it could have been an accident. We are not sure of all the details yet, but it seems that when the pilot whom he chartered in London was refuelling at Belgrade, the Count went into the buffet for some refreshment. While he was there, some one came in and told him that his pilot had been taken ill, but there was no need for him to worry because he had made arrangements for him to be taken on by some one else. Without any suspicion in his mind my uncle got back into the machine. The English pilot was not there, but there was another man whom he did not know in the cockpit. Naturally, he assumed it was the substitute for his own pilot. The machine at once took off and flew to Shavros, the capital of Lovitzna, where my uncle has been detained pending inquiries. It is said that his papers are not in order, which is, of course, absolute nonsense. The fact is, he is being held a prisoner, a hostage.'

'How do you know all this?'

'The Lovitznian government has given us official notice that the Count has been detained, and one of our agents in Shavros supplied the details.'

102

Biggles bit his lip. 'The whole thing was a plant, of course. Your uncle was tricked – kidnapped.'

'There is no doubt of it.'

'This is very awkward.'

'Awkward! It's terrible! Anything can happen to the Count now he's in Lovitzna.'

'I realize that, but it's no use losing our heads.'

'What can we do?'

'We've got to get him back.'

'That's impossible.'

Biggles turned a disapproving eye to Ludwig's pale face. 'I've told you before about using that word,' he admonished him.

'But how can we get him?'

'I've no idea,' confessed Biggles frankly. 'I've hardly had time to think yet, have I? Let us have a cigarette and see if we can work something out. This all comes of spies tapping your lines of communication,' he went on as he led the way into the wood. 'The enemy Intelligence Service must be very efficient or it couldn't have known that your uncle was on the way here. I think I know how it's been done, too.' He took from Smyth the map that had been found in the Lovitznian machine. 'Do you know anything about this place?' he asked, opening the map and laying a finger on the small area marked off in red.

Ludwig looked at the point indicated. 'Why, that's Bethstein's hunting-box*,' he exclaimed.

Biggles nodded. 'I thought it might be something like that,' he muttered. 'I shouldn't be surprised if there is a landing-ground there. We'll attend to that in due course; we haven't time now. We must get the Count home before

* Small house for use during the hunting season, usually in a remote area.

we do anything else.' Biggles sat down on an empty oil-drum, and stared thoughtfully at the ground. Algy and Ginger found seats near him. Ludwig remained standing.

It was a quarter of an hour before Biggles spoke again. 'I can think of only one way,' he said at last, slowly. 'It's risky, and, I fear, difficult, but I can think of nothing else.'

'What is it?' asked Ludwig, tersely.

Biggles glanced up. 'As an officer of the Maltovian army, and almost a member of the Cabinet, you had better know nothing about it. I'm going to ask you for a little assistance, though. I shall need two things.'

'What are they?'

'First, the name of a reliable Maltovian agent, or spy, in Shavros; I expect there is one. I shall also need the password, or whatever is necessary to gain his confidence. The second thing is a couple of suits of workmen's clothes – just ordinary peasants' coats and trousers.'

'There will be no difficulty about either, I think. When do you want these things?'

'Now. Just as soon as you can let me have them.'

'But it is dark.'

'That's why I want them now; I couldn't do much in daylight.'

'You're not – thinking of going to Shavros?'

'We shan't get your uncle home by sitting here, shall we?'

'But they will shoot you as spies.'

'If they catch us.'

'Did you blow up the bridge?'

'I did.'

'Then you can't get across the river.'

'I shan't need a bridge the way I am going.'

'You mean – you are going to fly?'

'How we are going needn't worry you, Ludwig. You trot

off and get those things I asked for and bring them back here as quickly as you can. We'll be getting ready. How long will it take you, do you think?'

'Half an hour – not more.'

'Then go to it. Time is precious. We've got to be back here by daylight, or we may not come back at all. Off you go, and, above all, keep your lips as tight as an oyster. No one must know anything about this. Not a soul – you understand? Nevertheless, if you can find out exactly where your uncle is being housed, it will help us a lot.'

Ludwig drew a deep breath, opened his mouth as if to say something, changed his mind and departed without a word. A minute later the others heard his car speeding up the road.

Algy spat out a pine needle which he had been chewing. 'Am I correct in supposing that we are going to spend the midnight hours fooling about in Lovitzna, instead of sleeping quietly in our beds?'

'You are,' replied Biggles briefly.

'What's the scheme?'

'I haven't got one yet, although there is a glimmering of something at the back of my mind. Our actions will be guided to a considerable extent by whether Ludwig is able to find out where the Count is being held.'

'Hadn't we better snatch a meal before we start? I have a suspicion that it may be some time before we get another.'

'Good idea.' Biggles turned to Smyth. 'Have you got any food down here, Smyth?'

'There's some cold stuff, sir – a pie, bread and cheese, and–'

'That'll do. Trot it out. We haven't time to go into the city. And start getting the big machine ready for the air.'

'Very good, sir.'

While they were eating Biggles explained his plan as far as it was possible. This was, briefly, that they should fly over in the big machine and land in a suitable field; one of them would remain in charge of the machine while the other two entered Shavros in the guise of peasants in the hope of effecting the rescue of the Count and bringing him back to the aeroplane.

'The weakest part of that scheme seems to be having the machine on the ground all that time,' replied Algy. 'If we land anywhere near Shavros it seems to me that somebody is bound to spot it. What then?'

Biggles rubbed his chin. 'It's a big risk, I must admit,' he confessed. 'We might be away for hours.'

'Whoever goes after the Count might not get back before daylight.'

'That's true.'

'I think it would be better if we employed the scheme used for spies in the old days, in France. Let two of us be landed and the other one take straight off again, returning from time to time until he gets the OK signal to land and pick the others up.'

'That's sound reasoning, but I think I can do it better than that,' went on Biggles. 'Let us compromise and put it this way. We all go over in the machine. Ginger and I will go into Shavros. You, Algy, will stay with the machine and wait on the ground as long as you are undiscovered. If you are spotted, or anything untoward occurs making it risky to remain in the field, you will take off and go home, returning every so often until you get a signal from us. If it is still dark we will signal three flashes on a torch; if it is daylight you will see us waving.'

'That's better,' agreed Algy.

'I think I can improve on that, too,' put in Ginger. 'Why run the risk of landing near the town? The farther away, the less will be the chances of discovery. Why not go to the field we landed in this afternoon? We know exactly where it is and we know that it has a good surface.'

'But that's miles away. We shouldn't get to Shavros before daylight, much less get there and back,' declared Biggles.

'You would, by going my way.'

'How's that?'

'Let's take Smyth's motorbike. He's got one on which he goes backwards and forwards to the city. There will be plenty of room for it in the machine. You can ride it and take me on the back *à la* pillion.'

'And how are we going to get the Count back to the machine? We can't expect one motorbike to carry three people.'

Ginger looked nonplussed for a moment, then he brightened. 'I've got it!' he cried. 'We could pinch a car. Or maybe the agent could get us one.'

'Yes, that might be possible,' agreed Biggles. 'There are drawbacks either way, but I'm inclined to agree with you that, taking things all round, it would be safer to land down in that wild part of the country where the field is than near Shavros. All right; if every one has finished eating we will see about getting the motorbike on board.'

They soon found that there was no difficulty about this, for, like nearly all modern heavy bombers, the big machine was provided with a cabin door for the convenience of the crew. The motorcycle was lashed in an upright position, this work being just completed as Ludwig returned, staggering under a heavy bundle.

'Here are the clothes,' he said, dropping the bundle on the ground.

'Then we'll get into them right away,' declared Biggles. 'You needn't bother to change, Algy, as you won't be leaving the machine. Did you get the other thing I asked for, Ludwig?'

'Yes.' Ludwig dropped his voice to a whisper. 'Go to the secondhand shop at the corner of the Stretta Barowsky and the main square. The man's name is Gustav; he sells all sorts of junk – old clothes, old hardware, and all that sort of thing. He also sells cigarettes and tobacco. Go in and ask for a packet of *Cigaretten Greta*, – he'll understand. That is the password. There is no such brand of cigarettes. If the shop is shut you will have to go to the side door.'

'Does he speak English?'

'A little, I believe. In any case, he speaks German and French.'

'That will be all right then. Many thanks, Ludwig; you'd better get off now. if you don't know what we are going to do you can't be held responsible for anything that may happen if our plans go wrong.'

'I have one more piece of news for you.'

'You found out where the Count—?'

'Yes.'

'Splendid! That will halve our difficulties. Where is he?'

'In the Hotel Grande. But he is watched.'

'Where is the hotel?'

'In the main square, not very far from Gustav's shop.'

'Good, then we'll get off.'

'How shall I know when you are back?'

'You'll have to wait until you hear from us. We'll let you know as quickly as we can.'

'Very well. Then I will return to the palace. Some one whom I need not name asks me to wish you God-speed in your venture. She will pray for your success and your safety.'

'Tell her that our task is made the easier for her kind thoughts,' returned Biggles quietly. 'Au revoir, Ludwig.'

'Goodbye. I—'

'Well?'

'I think you are very brave men,' blurted Ludwig.

Biggles smiled. 'Tush, man. It's merely a national habit.'

'What is?'

'Duty to those we serve and finishing the job we start on. We'll be seeing you.'

Biggles turned to the big machine as Ludwig disappeared into the darkness. 'Let's get away,' he said briefly. 'You and Carter will have to stick around, Smyth, to put flares out for us, or for Mr Lacey if he has to come back alone.'

'Very good, sir.'

'Got your pistol, Algy?'

'Yes.'

'And you, Ginger?'

'You bet I have.'

'Then be careful what you're doing with it. We'd better get these togs on,' he added, turning over the clothes which Ludwig had brought. 'You can be starting up, Algy.'

Five minutes later the big machine roared up into the night.

Chapter 13

In Enemy Country

It was not an ideal night for flying. When they took off the sky was, admittedly, fairly clear, but as they droned northward, climbing all the time for altitude, the open patches became smaller as high cloud drifted down from the direction in which the machine was heading.

'I don't like the look of that stuff,' declared Biggles to Algy, who was sitting beside him.

Algy looked down at the vast, blue-black shadow that was Maltovia. Ahead, a thin grey ribbon wandered roughly at right angles across their course. 'Visibility is still fairly good,' he opined. 'I can see the river ahead. We ought to have no difficulty in finding the field.'

'It won't be so easy later on if this cloud thickens,' returned Biggles grimly. 'I smell a change in the weather. It was fairly clear when we started, for which reason I hardly took the weather into consideration. It's getting colder, too. If it starts to rain, we shall be in ice-forming* conditions before we get back.'

Nothing more was said. At twelve thousand feet, while they were still some seven or eight miles from the river, Biggles cut out the engines and began a long glide towards the frontier, his idea being, of course, to enter the enemy country unremarked.

---

* If ice forms on wings, engines or control surfaces of a plane, it can force it down, causing a crash landing.

'If I can get her down without using the engines again no one should be any the wiser,' he observed as he strained his eyes into the gloom beyond the river, trying to pick up the field on which they had landed earlier in the day.

'I can see it! There it is, slightly to the left,' called Algy, who had opened a side window and was gazing down at the silent earth. 'There is no one about by the look of it; there isn't a light for miles except the headlights of a car on the road about five miles away.'

'Fine!' declared Biggles, beginning to sideslip* gently towards the field on which he now fixed his eyes.

Slowly, the big machine dropped lower and lower, silent except for the faint hum of wind in the wires. A slow S turn brought the nose of the machine in line with the landing-ground, and a minute later the wheels were running over the soft turf. The machine ran to a standstill not far from the hedge.

'Good! That's that,' murmured Biggles with a sigh of thankfulness as he switched off, for such a landing as the one he had just made is always a strain on the nerves.

Ginger was already untying the motorcycle by the time the others joined him in the cabin, and a few minutes saw the little surface vehicle standing under the wing of the machine that had brought it.

'All right, Algy, we'll get off,' announced Biggles. 'You know what to do. Stand by as long as things are quiet, but if there is trouble beat it for home. If you have to go, watch the whole area when you come back in case for any unseen reason we cannot reach this particular field. Three flashes on the torch will locate us; it will also mean that you can

* A sideways movement of an aircraft used in this case to lose altitude quickly.

111

get down where you see the flashes. If we are not back here by dawn, go home, and you'll have to use your discretion as to what to do after that. If you come back again after daylight watch for a white handkerchief being waved. Is that all clear?'

'Perfectly.'

'Cheerio, then.'

'Best of luck.'

Biggles pushed the motorbike off its stand and began to wheel it towards the road which ran along the northern edge of the field. Ginger pushed from behind. It was by no means an easy task, particularly as they took some time to find a gap through the hedge, which was tangled and overgrown, but in the end they managed it and stood on the road, which they now saw was in a shocking state of disrepair.

'It doesn't look as though this part of the country is used very much, does it?' murmured Ginger, as he switched on the headlight.

'No, it's a pretty wild spot,' agreed Biggles as he started the engine. 'Get aboard.'

Ginger blew on his hands as he straddled the luggage bracket. 'I fancy we are going to find it a bit chilly by the time we get to Shavros,' he said. 'OK, Chief, let her go.'

As the motorbike with its two riders moved down the road with gradually increasing speed, Biggles knew that they had started on one of the most difficult and dangerous tasks they had ever undertaken; but he kept his thoughts to himself.

It seemed to Ginger that they were hours getting to Shavros. Actually, they covered the forty miles to the Lovitznian capital in about an hour and a half. The machine was capable of greater speed, but the roads were in a bad state, and Biggles pursued a policy of slow but sure. They met two or three cars, and an occasional wayfarer, none of whom caused them any anxiety or alarm. One or two pedestrians called out what was evidently the Lovitznian equivalent of 'Goodnight', to which Biggles, not being able to speak the language, could only grunt a reply.

But with their arrival in Shavros he knew that their difficulties might begin at any moment, and here again their greatest handicap was ignorance of the language. For this reason he dared not park the motorcycle in a garage, although they saw more than one, both in the outskirts of the city and in the main streets through which they presently passed. Finally, he left it in what looked like a public parking place in the big square in the centre of the town, where several cars were standing, one or two with chauffeurs and the others empty.

'This looks like the place where we get our car when we want one,' murmured Ginger, in a low voice, as he cast an appraising eye over the vehicles.

'It will be time to think about that when we get what we came for,' answered Biggles quietly. 'Let us see if we can find Gustav.'

They had no difficulty in finding the secondhand shop, but it was closed, the time now being nearly ten o'clock. A knock on the side door, however, produced a little, wizened old man with watery eyes and a furtive manner. He eyed the two 'peasants' suspiciously.

'Gustav?' questioned Biggles softly.

'*Ja.*'

'*Einige Zigaretten Greta, bitte*,*' murmured Biggles softly.

The old man started slightly. '*Herein**,*' he muttered,

---

* German: some Greta cigarettes, please.
** German: come in.

and stood aside to allow them to enter, after which he led the way to a small sitting-room.

'Do you speak English?' asked Biggles curtly.

'A leedle, yes.'

Biggles took a plunge, knowing that he had either to trust the man entirely or not at all. 'Tell me what you know of Count Stanhauser,' he demanded. 'We have come to fetch him.'

Briefly, in broken and often halting English, Gustav repeated the story Ludwig had already told them.

'In what part of the hotel is he?' asked Biggles, when he had finished.

'Der room twenty-von.'

'On what floor is that?'

'You mean – der stairs?'

'Yes.'

'Der second.'

'Is he free? I mean, is he allowed to walk about?'

'Yes, but always der two men watch.'

'Is it possible to get a message to him?'

'The old man shook his head. 'Nein – nod possible. In time it could be arrange, perhaps yes, but tonight, no.'

'Well, we can't hang about here until the morning.' Biggles looked at Ginger. Ginger looked at Biggles.

'Bit awkward, isn't it?' he said.

Biggles did not answer. For a minute or two he stared into space, turning over the problem in his mind. At last he drew a deep breath. 'I want to avoid anything dramatic, if it is possible,' he said slowly. 'Simplicity is the key-note of success in this sort of thing.' He turned to Gustav. 'Do you happen to have a lorry?' he asked.

'Lorry? What is dot?'

'A big motor-car for carrying luggage.'

'No.'

114

'Pity. Could you get one?'

'Not at dis hour. Tomorrow – perhaps.'

'Forget about tomorrow. I am only concerned with to-night.'

'I have big hand-truck in der yard – der ting I vetch my cases from der station.'

'That's better. Do you happen to have an old blouse amongst your stock, a blouse such as the porters wear, and a cap?'

'You want to look like porter – *ja*?'

'Yes.'

The old man disappeared into the shop, and presently returned with a loose blue linen blouse and a peaked cap. Biggles put them on; they did not fit very well, but well enough. 'Get me a suitcase,' he ordered.

'Big or liddle? I 'ave many.'

'Better bring a big one.'

Again the old man rummaged in his shop and came back with the desired article.

Biggles smiled. 'Good!' he said. 'Now we are getting on. Gustav, I want you to load up on your truck all the glass and crockery you've got in the shop.'

The old man stared.

'All right, you'll be paid for it,' Biggles told him.

'What you do wid it?'

'Break it.'

'Break—'

'Listen. This is the plan. I want the cart piled high, as high as you can get it, with anything that will break when it falls over. Ginger, this is what I want you to do. I want you to wheel the truck past the hotel. When you get opposite the main entrance it will get out of hand, run into the gutter, and turn over. The idea is to make a noise.'

115

'And attract every eye within a hundred yards to the fool who did the damage?' put in Ginger. 'Thank you kindly.'

'That's the idea. You've hit the nail absolutely on the head. When you unload those crocks on to the pavement I'll warrant everyone within earshot will dash up to see what it's all about. What is more important, every one in the vestibule of the hotel will run out. It isn't in human nature to resist. As they dash out I shall walk in, and I'll bet you not a single soul will see me go. But don't you worry about me. All you will have to do after you have upset the applecart – I mean the crock cart – is to get across to the other side of the square and stand by an empty car ready for a quick get-away. As soon as you see me and the Count coming, jump in, start up, and be ready to put your foot down.'

'Is that all?' inquired Ginger, with a hint of sarcasm in his voice.

'That's all.'

'It should be enough to go on with, too,' muttered Ginger. 'OK. Let's start loading up the glassware. All my life I've wanted to hear a load of glass fall on a stone pavement, but I've never been able to afford it.'

'Your wish is about to come true, and what is more, it's going to cost you nothing – not a bean,' grinned Biggles. 'Come on, Gustav, let's get busy.'

The old man raised a half-hearted protest at this proposed wilful destruction of his entire stock, but Biggles waved him to silence. 'Think of what is at stake,' he reproved him, as they made their way through to a yard at the back of the house.

Ginger laughed quietly once or twice as the load of crockery and glass rose higher and higher on the truck.

'Go ahead,' invited Biggles. 'Now is the time to laugh.

116

The noise this little lot will make when it hits the concrete is going to surprise you, and there won't be any time for laughing then.'

'This must be what they call going out for a grand slam.'

Biggles smiled. 'That's it.'

In about twenty minutes the load was complete, and Ginger eyed it nervously.

'I feel as if I was about to commit a murder,' he confessed.

'I'll commit one if you spill these plates in the wrong place,' Biggles told him seriously. 'Watch how you go. Give me a minute to get across.' He picked up the suitcase. 'Goodbye, Gustav, in case I don't see you again,' he said. 'When I get back I'll let them know how useful you've been.' With that, he opened the gates of the yard and walked boldly towards the hotel. Halfway across the square he looked back and saw Ginger following. Reaching the pavement, he took up a position a few yards from the hotel entrance and there awaited events.

He had not long to wait. Ginger came striding across the square with his fragile load swaying dangerously. It was clear that the whole thing might go over at any moment. Ginger evidently realized it, for he suddenly swung the vehicle round and deliberately charged the pavement in front of the hotel. The pile was already toppling before the wheels hit the kerb, and the few passers-by scattered when they saw what was about to happen.

The crash far surpassed anything Biggles had imagined. He was, for a moment, stunned, and with the mighty crash still ringing in his ears he could only stare at the ruin, while mugs, jugs, pots, and glasses continued to dribble out of the over-turned hand-cart; unbroken plates

117

and saucers bowled down the pavement and crashed into the railings, or fell into the gutter.

There was a moment of silence, as if every one within earshot had held his breath. Then uproar followed. People ran from all directions; windows were thrown open; the swing doors of the hotel were flung aside as the hall porter, attendants, and visitors who had been standing in the vestibule poured out. The sight brought Biggles back to normal. Picking up the suitcase, he walked calmly up the steps and entered the hotel. One glance showed him that the vestibule was empty. Straight across it he walked to the stairs which he could see on the other side. As he went up he met several people running down, for the lift-boy had joined the crowd on the pavement, but he took no notice of them. He did not even pause at the first-floor landing but went straight on up to the second. At the top a notice caught his eye. An arrow pointed to the left with the numbers 29–45. Another pointed to the right, 16–28. Biggles took the corridor indicated, eyes running swiftly over the numbers on the doors. Six paces brought him to the one he was looking for – number 21. Without hesitation he turned the handle and walked in.

Three men were seated in the room, all in dark civilian clothes. One he recognized instantly. It was Count Stanhauser. The others were strangers and they sprang to their feet at the intrusion. Their movements ceased, however, when they found themselves staring into the muzzle of Biggles's automatic.

'Come on, sir,' said Biggles crisply.

The Count rose to his feet like a man sleep-walking.

'Come along, sir, hurry up,' called Biggles peremptorily.

The Count recovered himself with an effort, and thereafter he acted swiftly. As he walked through into the corridor Biggles took the key out of the inside of the door, backed out of the room and locked the door behind him.

'Follow me, and whatever happens, keep going. We've no time to talk now,' Biggles told the Count as he put the pistol in his pocket and set off towards the stairs.

They went down the first flight without meeting a soul, but on the next landing they almost collided with a man who had evidently just come in through the vestibule. Biggles was about to pass when he caught the other's eyes. They both stopped dead. Recognition was mutual and instantaneous. It was Zarovitch, the Lovitznian minister who had visited them in their rooms in London on the night when Count Stanhauser had first called.

Biggles's hand jerked to his pocket, but before he could prevent him, the Lovitznian had turned, and, yelling at the top of his voice, was going down the stairs three at a time.

'That should set things buzzing,' growled Biggles. 'What is he saying?'

'He is shouting for the police.'

'In that case we had better find another way out. Let's try this passage.' Biggles hurried along a corridor, but after taking several turnings it came to an end. The corridor was a cul-de-sac. Shouts and the sound of running footsteps reached their ears.

'We are lost,' declared the Count with bitter fatality.

'Never say that,' returned Biggles coldly. A flat double door caught his eye, and he recognized it for a service lift, the sort that is used for heavy luggage. But the lift itself was not there. He pressed the call-button and heard a bell jangle somewhere below. Would it be answered? He realized that everything now depended upon that. A moment later there was a grating jar as the lift doors were slammed somewhere below. Then came the peculiar

119

electric hum of an ascending elevator. At the same moment Zarovitch, with several men, some in uniform, appeared round the corner of the corridor. They pulled up dead when they looked into Biggles's gun.

'One more step, Zarovitch, and it will be your last,' called Biggles crisply, the last word being cut short by the crash of the lift doors as they were thrown open.

A yawning porter stepped into the corridor, but his jaws snapped together and his eyes bulged as he took in the scene.

Biggles swept him aside with a swift movement of his arm. 'In you go,' he told the Count shortly.

There was a rush of footsteps as he slammed the doors. He pressed the bottom button and the lift started going down. 'The question is, where is this going to land us?' he murmured, as he put the pistol in his pocket and waited expectantly for the exit to appear.

It came, and revealed a large, dimly-lit room, littered with trunks and suitcases. 'Looks like the reception dump,' said Biggles as his eyes flashed round the room, seeking the door. Finding it, he reached it in a few brisk strides and threw it open. A courtyard, with access to a side street, met his gaze, but it was not this that made him falter, speechlessly. Everything was covered with a mantle of white. It was snowing steadily.

Chapter 14

Fresh Dangers

'What are we waiting for?' asked the Count anxiously.

Biggles took a fresh grip of himself. He laughed harshly.
'Nothing,' he said, as he stepped forward. 'Funny how the
one thing you don't think of so often happens to trip you
up, isn't it?' he added bitterly.

'Why, what has happened?'

'I'll tell you later. Let's go.'

As Biggles expected, the side street brought them to the
main square, now nearly deserted. A few curious spectators were still lingering by the wreck of Gustav's stock-
in-trade, but he paid no attention to them as he cut
straight across the square to where the cars had been. He
increased his pace as he saw that only three remained, and
in one of these a chauffeur was making ready to depart.
Ginger was leaning against a tree near one of the others,
but he was evidently on the alert, for as soon as he saw
Biggles coming he slipped inside the nearest car, and by
the time the others had reached him the engine was
running.

'Step on it,' snapped Biggles as the car moved forward.

'You were a long time,' grumbled Ginger. 'I don't mind
telling you I began to get worried when the cars started
going. Originally, I chose a Mercedes—'

'Never mind what you chose; look where you're going,'
interrupted Biggles curtly.

'Where are we going, anyway?'

'Back to the machine, of course.'

'The machine doesn't look like being much good to us even if it's still there,' answered Ginger, peering between the flakes of snow that were being caught by the windscreen.

'The snow may stop.'

Ginger shook his head. 'Not it. Not yet, anyway. I saw it start; nice big gentle flakes, as if it was going to make a really good job of it.'

'Well, we've nowhere else to go,' answered Biggles. 'It would choose this moment to start, confound it.' He turned to the Count. 'We've got an aeroplane waiting out in the country,' he explained. 'But, as you may know, an aeroplane isn't exactly a safe conveyance in a snow-storm, even if it can get off the ground – and it can't always do that.'

'Is there no other way of getting into Maltovia?' asked the Count.

'None.'

'You might try the bridge.'

'We might, but it wouldn't be much use.'

'Why not?'

'The two middle arches are missing.'

'*What!*'

'The most important part of the bridge, which is the middle, is no longer there.'

'Where is it?'

'In the river.'

'Great heavens! How did it get there?'

'It got in the way of a lump of high explosive and came off second best.'

'How on earth did that happen?'

'It didn't exactly happen. I dropped a bomb on it. The Lovitznians were getting ready to march across.'

'Ah! I see.'

'Had I known what I know now I would have waited until tomorrow, but we didn't know you were a prisoner when we bombed the bridge.'

'What are we going to do, then?'

'Whatever happens, I think we must go to the aircraft, or, at least, to the place where we left it, in case Algy is still standing by – not that I think he will be. I hope he had the sense to clear off home when the snow started.'

'Would he be able to do that?'

'Yes; the snow is coming from the north. Janovica lies to the south. If he took off at once he could race the snow home. But there, it isn't much use guessing; we shall do better to wait and see what has happened before we make any plans. Take it steadily, Ginger. We shan't see the ruts in this snow, and we only need to break a back axle now to be in a really good mess.'

After that they fell silent while Ginger made the best time he could, with safety, back to the landing-field. They did it in little over an hour, by which time the snow was almost blinding in its intensity. When Biggles stepped out of the car on arrival at their destination he sank in it up to his knees. 'It's worse than I thought,' he muttered savagely.

'Is he here?' asked Ginger, referring, apparently, to Algy.

'I don't know. You can't see ten yards in this stuff. Even if he is, flying is out of the question. I'm prepared to take risks, but I never did see any sense in committing suicide.'

Leaving the car on the side of the road, they hurried across the field to where they had left the machine, but, as Biggles had fully expected, it had gone. It mattered little, for he knew that it could not have taken off in two feet of snow.

'And now what?' asked Ginger resignedly, when they had made quite sure that the machine was not there.

It was the Count who came to the rescue with a new hope. 'Wait a minute!' he cried. 'I believe I have the answer. I know this part of the country well, because I used to fish in the river when I was a boy. There is an old mill some distance down the stream; in the old days they used to keep a boat there.'

'How far is this place?'

'It must be nearly four miles from here.'

'As far as that! Can we get to it in the car?'

'No, we must follow the river. There is a tow-path, you know.'

'It should be a pleasant little jaunt on a night like this,' replied Biggles, sarcastically. 'I haven't much use for walking at the best of times, but in this stuff, and at this hour – still, it's no use grumbling, I suppose. Do you feel able to walk four miles, Count?'

'Yes, I think I can do that.'

'Very well. We may as well start as stand here and freeze to death.'

They set off in a straight line for the river, or as near a straight line as they could keep, for walking through the whirling flakes was no easy matter. Half an hour brought them to the tow-path, and Ginger could not help reflecting that they had covered the same ground in one minute of time earlier in the evening. The river lay like a great black snake in the snow so they could not lose their way, while the hard foundation of the path made the going easier than it had been over the turf.

The Count turned to the right on reaching the river and then set off along the bank. 'The snow has its advantages,' he observed optimistically. 'We need hardly fear pursuit.'

'I should have been still less afraid of pursuit with a

joystick in my fist,' replied Biggles grimly. 'However, we are not doing so badly.'

Thereafter they kept their breath for the task on hand, but even so they were all nearly exhausted when, two hours later, the Count announced that they were nearing their objective. He declared that he recognized a bend in the river. Thus cheered, the little party moved on again, thankful at least that the exertion kept them fairly warm.

'We've got a dickens of a long walk in front of us even when we get across the river,' observed Ginger.

'We shall find a conveyance of some sort as soon as we get into Maltovia,' stated the Count confidently.

'In any case, it was no use staying in Lovitzna,' put in Biggles. 'Even if it was a thousand miles to Janovica, thanks to this snow we have no alternative to what we are doing.'

'That is true,' agreed the Count, brushing the worst of the snow from his clothes. Fortunately, it was the dry, crisp sort that did not cling and melt. 'Ah, I see where we are,' he went on. 'I remember this place quite well.'

The snow had thinned somewhat, and the others could just make out high, wild-looking, pine-clad slopes on either side of them. The open country had been left behind and they were, in fact, passing through a deep valley.

'What on earth would a mill be doing in such a place?' asked Biggles, mystified.

'It is a saw-mill,' replied the Count. 'The trees are cut down and shipped by barges to the other side of the country, where they are sawn into lengths for pit-props. There are some mines there. We must go carefully; it will not do to be discovered; the people who own the mill are Lovitznians, don't forget. Ah! there is the mill. I see it. I—' The Count's voice died away curiously. 'It seems to have changed,' he added dubiously after a moment or two.

125

They took a few paces nearer.

'I don't want to be pessimistic, but it looks to me as if all that is left of your mill is charred stumps,' observed Biggles casually. 'The place has been burnt down.'

The Count uttered a low cry and ran forward to where a few rough planks spanned a backwater. 'You are right,' he cried. 'The place has been burnt down, and – the boat has gone.'

Biggles stopped on the planks regarding the desolate scene. Where the saw-mill had stood, a gaunt skeleton of charred beams loomed darkly against the sky. In the backwater, half submerged in mud, lay an old barge, rotten, derelict. Near the water were piles of fir trees, stripped of their branches. 'It looks as if we've arrived about five years too late,' he murmured evenly.

'I'm afraid so,' agreed the Count sadly.

Ginger drew a deep breath and was about to speak when a long, mournful howl welled up somewhere in the black pinewood beside the river. He shivered. 'My goodness! What's that?' he cried.

The Count began to back away. 'Wolves!' he said in a startled voice.

'Wolves!' Biggles almost barked the word. 'Do you have wolves here?'

'They come down in packs from Siberia in the winter. Cold and hunger drive them down.'

'How very cheerful,' answered Biggles, peering into the darkness, at the same time taking out his automatic. 'I don't want them to satisfy their hunger on me, if it can be prevented,' he announced.

'Nor me,' declared Ginger vehemently.

At that moment the snow stopped, the sky cleared like magic, and a wan moon shed a pallid light over the whitened world.

'Well, what are we going to do?' asked Biggles sharply. 'Think of something somebody. The situation is getting a bit beyond me.'

'Look!' The Count almost hissed the word. Swinging round, the others saw that he was facing the way they had come, evidently with the idea of returning. Fifty yards away, in the middle of the path, several dark shapes were slinking.

Biggles levelled his pistol, but before he could fire, almost as if the wolves had divined his intention, the shapes had merged into the black background of the trees.

The Count began walking quickly towards the mill. 'Let us take refuge in here,' he said. 'The brutes may think twice before attacking what is, or what looks like, a building. If they catch us in the open we shall not have a chance.'

The others needed no second invitation. Stumbling over logs and fallen timber, they made their way as fast as they could into what was left of the mill. The ground floor was piled up high with debris, but from one corner of it a flight of stone steps led upwards to the few boards that remained of the first floor.

'We had better get up there until we decide what we are going to do,' suggested Biggles.

'Yes, that is our best plan,' agreed the Count. 'It looks as if we shall have to wait here until the morning. Wolves are cowardly brutes and seldom show themselves in daylight.'

'Well, we shan't have long to wait, there is that about it,' replied Biggles, glancing at his wrist-watch. 'It's turned five o'clock now.'

They made their way up the tottering steps until they stood on the remains of the first floor. Biggles looked through the ruins of what had once been a wall. Sitting in

127

a circle round the building were thirty or forty grey wolves, panting, with lolling tongues. Their breath rose up like a cloud of steam. 'Pretty lot of little fellows, aren't they?' He said to Ginger, who had joined him.

Ginger did not answer. He was drawing his pistol.

'What are you going to do?' asked Biggles.

'Have a crack at the swines,' replied Ginger vindictively.

'It will be time enough to do that when they start coming up the stairs,' Biggles told him bluntly. 'Save your ammunition. In any case, we don't want to tell the world where we are.'

'This is what comes of leaving good old England,' muttered Ginger morosely.

'Well, you said you were craving for some excitement. You're getting it, so I don't see what you've got to grumble about,' Biggles told him shortly, as he sat down to wait for the dawn.

Chapter 15

A Perilous Undertaking

Slowly the moon sank and the sky cleared. The weather turned milder as the wind swung to another quarter; presently it died away altogether, and the mournful silence that settled over the dismal scene was broken only by the drip, drip, drip of melting snow.

Presently Ginger spoke. 'The wolves are coming nearer,' he said, with a hint of alarm in his voice.

Biggles stood up. The wolves were still sitting on their haunches, but several of them had edged appreciably nearer.

'That is their usual way,' said the Count, who was watching. 'They are waiting for one, more daring than the rest, to make a rush.'

'Then we'd better do something to discourage them before they start anything like that,' replied Biggles. 'I had hoped it would not be necessary to use our pistols in case the shots were heard, but we might as well be captured by the Lovitznians as chewed up by a mob of ravening wolves. Have a crack at them, Ginger.'

Ginger levelled his automatic, resting the muzzle on a charred beam; his finger tightened on the trigger and the weapon went off. For a second or two he was blinded by the flash, but when his sight adjusted itself again he saw that the wolves had all disappeared.

'Didn't I hit one?' he asked in a disappointed voice.

'No, but you made one jump,' grinned Biggles.

'They'll come back when they get over their fright,' declared the Count.

'Then they'll have to buck up if they aim to get a meal before morning,' replied Biggles. 'It's beginning to get light – look!' He pointed to the east where a grey streak was creeping up over the tree-clad hills. 'Incidentally, a quick thaw seems to have set in,' he continued. 'I'm afraid Algy won't know what to do for the best.'

'It will be no use him thinking of landing in that same field, even if the snow does melt,' put in the Count quickly.

'Why not?'

'Can't you imagine what happens when a fall of snow like this starts melting? All that low country is inundated.'

'My gosh! I never thought of that,' muttered Biggles. 'And what about the river?'

'The water will pour off the hills, and there will be such a spate that nothing will be able to get across the river, perhaps for some days.'

'One way or another we look like having a bonny time,' murmured Ginger disconsolately, casually throwing a piece of wood at the swiftly running stream.

'As soon as it gets properly light a hue and cry will start and we shall be chased up and down the country like escaped convicts,' growled Biggles. 'I suppose it is no use trying to swim across the river?'

'Absolutely out of the question,' declared the Count. 'Quite apart from the speed of the current, we should be frozen to death before we were half-way across.'

'Confound it! Surely there must be some way we can get across?'

Ginger suddenly grabbed Biggles's arm. 'There is!' he cried triumphantly.

'What do you mean?'

'You saw me throw that piece of wood in the river just now?'

'Yes.'

'Well, it's gone ashore on the opposite bank at the next bend, where that piece of sand sticks out. The current swings round this corner, hits the bank here and shoots right across to the other side at the next bend. Look, you can see the piece of wood I threw lying on the bank. With some of these tree trunks tied together we could soon have a raft strong enough to float us over to the other side. All we need is some rope.'

'Good work, Ginger,' cried Biggles enthusiastically. 'Let's see if we can find something that will do to tie the logs together. What about the barge? We might find something there. As it's light, I don't think we need worry about the wolves, but keep your gun handy in case of accidents.'

They all made their way down the steps, looking for anything that could possibly be used as a binding material. They found nothing in the mill itself, but on the deck of the barge Biggles pointed to an old tarpaulin. 'We could no doubt tear that into strips if we can find nothing else, although it would take a bit of tying. Or that,' he added, pointing to a length of chain. 'Rope would suit us better, of course.'

There was nothing else on the deck, but dragging open a mouldering locker in the bows Biggles gave a cry of delight, for lying in a mildewed heap were several odd lengths of rope. He picked up a piece, and made a grimace as, giving it a sharp jerk, it snapped like a piece of wet cotton.

'That won't hold much,' said the Count ruefully.

'If we handle it carefully it ought to be good enough to keep a few logs together for a few minutes,' replied Biggles.

'We'll thread the chain through the middle to take most of the strain.' So saying, he picked up an armful of the rope and hurried back to the pile of logs that lay nearest to the water's edge. They were, in fact, almost in the now rising water, ordinary fir trees of about six inches diameter, trimmed ready for transportation.

'Count, will you wind the rope round one end, while you, Ginger, tie the other end as I pass them down to you? Make an ordinary flat raft, keeping the logs as close together as you can. Ease them into the water as you go along, then we shall be able to test it until it will take our weight.'

It was a perfectly straightforward task, but one that demanded a certain amount of care on account of the rottenness of the ropes. For half an hour they worked feverishly, Biggles handing down the logs to the others, who then lashed them together at either end. The sun came out and they actually perspired as they worked.

'It must be nearly wide enough,' announced Biggles at last, pausing to look at the result of their labours. 'By James! We've no time to lose, either. Look at the river. It's risen a foot in the last half hour and it's travelling twice as fast as it was. Slip and get that length of chain, Ginger; we'll use it as a main bracing. We might have the tarpaulin, too, to throw over the top. What the—!' He broke off and swung round, staring up the river bank. 'I thought I heard somebody shout,' he said breathlessly.

'So did I,' said Ginger tersely. He ran into the mill and sped up the steps to take advantage of the elevation they provided. One look and he was down again, almost falling in his haste. 'Launch her, launch her!' he gasped.

'What is it?'

'Soldiers. Soldiers and bloodhounds. They're following

132

our trail. They are only just round the corner and they're coming at a run.'

Biggles wasted no more time in conversation. Taking one end of that part of the raft which still remained ashore, he dragged it towards the water, while the Count did the same thing on the other side. Ginger got behind and pushed, as much to take the strain off the ropes as for any other reason. In a moment the crude raft was floating on the stream, but under their combined weight it sagged frighteningly. Water surged up between the logs and over the outside edges.

'Lie flat, everybody,' ordered Biggles. 'We shall spread our weight that way.' So saying, he pushed the raft clear. Instantly the powerful current took it in its grip and it swung, turning round slowly, out into the stream.

They were less than halfway over, all watching the bend round which their pursuers would appear, when a hound, baying furiously, bounded round the corner. A moment later a soldier appeared, then another, and a shout told those on the raft that they had been seen.

'Heads down, everybody,' ordered Biggles quietly. 'They'll start shooting in a minute. We needn't get worried if they do; I've yet to meet a man who can fire a rifle with any sort of accuracy after he has been running.'

Hardly were the words past his lips when a rifle crashed and a line of spray zipped across the surface of the water about a yard from the raft. Biggles pulled out his pistol and returned the fire, more to upset the marksman's aim than from any real hope of hitting him. *Bang! Bang! Bang!* roared the weapon, and the several Lovitznians who had now appeared dived into the wood for cover. 'How far are we from the bank, Ginger?' he asked, with his eyes on the place where the Lovitznians had disappeared.

'Twenty yards.'

'Shall we go ashore on that spit of sand?'

'I think so.'

'Then jump for it everybody, as soon as we touch, and make a dash for cover. Swerve as you run and throw yourselves flat as soon as you are among the trees.'

An instant later there was a jar as the swiftly drifting raft struck the bank, and a violent lurch as somebody jumped ashore. Biggles could not see who it was. There was a ragged volley from the opposite bank and several bullets flicked up the water perilously near the raft. *Bang! Bang!* roared Biggles's weapon again as he fired at the flashes. Another lurch told him that the second passenger had jumped ashore and that he was now alone on the raft, so, after emptying his pistol at the enemy's position, he leapt ashore and darted, zigzagging as he ran, towards the trees. A bullet kicked up the sand near his feet; another whistled past his head and tore a long white splinter from the side of a tree, but he reached his objective untouched, and, flinging himself flat, wormed his way into the undergrowth. 'Are you all right?' he called anxiously.

Both Ginger and the Count answered him in the affirmative, and he relaxed with relief. 'Start working your way into the thickest of the trees, but take care not to show yourselves,' he ordered, and after allowing them to get a short start, he followed. There was plenty of cover, so the move was not really dangerous, and when, presently, he came to a fold in the hillside, he found the others sitting on a boulder, waiting for him.

'We were just about in time, weren't we?' He smiled at the Count, who seemed not in the least perturbed by the hardships and dangers he had undergone.

The Count nodded cheerfully. 'We're still in Lovitzna, though, don't forget,' he said warningly.

'How far are we from the frontier?'

'Not more than two miles, I think.'

'Good! Then if it's all the same to you, we'll push on. The sooner we are out of this country and into our own, the sooner shall I breathe freely. The terrain is flat on the other side of these hills, if I remember rightly, isn't it?'

'Yes, the ground falls away quickly to the central plain.'

'Then if we can get there, there is a chance that Algy may spot us and pick us up,' said Biggles thoughtfully. 'I expect he will be in the air by this time, looking for us – that is, if he got back all right,' he added a trifle anxiously.

It was a steep pull up the hill and it took them nearly an hour to reach the top. The river was somewhere below them but they could not see it owing to the trees, nor could they hear any sounds of pursuit. A few minutes' rest to regain their breath and they started off again, now travelling downhill. Another twenty minutes brought them to the frontier, an ordinary barbed-wire fence, but no one was in sight. If there was a frontier patrol they did not see it, so they lost no time in climbing over the fence into their own country.

'That's better,' announced Biggles, as they set off again, plunging down the tree-clad slopes towards the open plain.

They had not been going very long when the sound of an aircraft was borne to their ears.

'That's Algy!' cried Ginger delightedly.

Biggles shook his head as his practised ear took in the note of the engines, now rapidly drawing nearer. 'You're wrong,' he said. 'Look!' He pointed up through the tree-tops as a formation of scouts raced low overhead. They carried the brown crosses of Lovitzna, and on the leader's wing-struts were small triangular pennants. 'Looking for us, I'll be bound,' he added. 'Well, they'll be clever if they spot us among these trees.'

'What about when we get in the open?' asked Ginger.

'Let's wait until we get there,' returned Biggles evenly.

They saw the enemy machines several times as they went on down the slope. There was no doubt as to their object, but, as Biggles had said, there was little reason to fear that they would be seen, and even if they were it was difficult to know what the aircraft could do, for the hillside was certainly no place for a landing.

'The only thing that worries me is that Algy might come beetling over looking for us and run into this tribe of cut-throats,' murmured Biggles, nodding towards the Lovitznian formation which could just be seen in the distance.

'I was thinking the same thing,' answered Ginger moodily, as they hurried on down the steep incline.

After that little more was said. It took them the best part of an hour to reach the open country beyond the foothills; in fact, during that time only one observation was made, and that was when a machine, obviously a two-seater, sailed over at a tremendous height. 'It looks as if they're bringing out their entire air force to look for us,' remarked Biggles, as he glanced upwards.

'I think I can see a farm-house over there,' put in the Count. 'We might make our way towards it in the hope of begging something to eat and a cup of tea or coffee. They will hardly refuse us that when they learn who we are.'

'That sounds a sensible idea to me,' agreed Biggles warmly.

Increasing their pace, they set off towards the homestead, pushing their way through a hedge and cutting across a wide field as the shortest way. Thus it came about that they were right in the open and a good hundred yards from the nearest cover when the patrol leader of the enemy formation suddenly skimmed low over the hills immediately behind them.

Biggles realized the danger instantly, for there was no question as to whether or not they would be seen. The enemy pilots were obviously still looking for them, although the formation had broken up, possibly with the object of covering more ground, and the man in the brown-crossed fighter had now only to look down to see the fugitives, outlined clearly against the white background of swiftly melting snow.

Biggles had jerked to a standstill as the machine came into view. For a moment he stared at it while he summed up the situation. Then he started running back towards the nearest point of the hedge, where, having crossed it, he knew there was a ditch. 'Come on, he shouted, for he knew by the manner in which the nose of the enemy machine dropped suddenly that they had been seen.

They were still ten yards from the hedge when the harsh rattle of machine-guns cut clear above the increasing roar of the engine, and a stream of bullets sent snow and turf leaping into the air. It stirred them to frantic efforts, and they all flung themselves pell-mell into the ditch as the fighter zoomed over them, its wheels not more than a few yards over their heads.

'Get flat in the bottom of the ditch,' yelled Biggles frantically. 'Never mind the snow. This fellow means business.'

He heard the machine scream round and come racing back, and a glance showed him that the pilot was doing what he feared he would; not that he expected otherwise, for he knew from his own experience that they were dealing with a man who understood his business. Instead of flying across the ditch as he had on the first occasion, he was now getting into a position from which he could fly straight along it, enfilading it with a raking fire for its entire length in the manner adopted by trench-strafing pilots during the war. Yet there was nothing they could do, and Biggles knew it. Their only chance was to remain where they were, although it seemed more than likely that one or all of them would be hit; yet to forsake the ditch for the open would only make that more certain.

It was at this moment, while Biggles was racking his brains for some solution to the desperate problem with which they were faced, that he became vaguely aware of a change in the situation. The information was not conveyed to him by his eyes, for he had wedged himself as tightly as he could into the black mud at the bottom of the ditch. It was the noise that told him something had happened, for it seemed suddenly to swell to an incredible volume, as if the pilot was deliberately flying his machine straight into the ground. For perhaps three seconds his guns chattered, the bullets thudding into the ground and smashing through the hedge; then they, too, seemed to rise to an ear-splitting crescendo, as if half a dozen guns instead of two were firing. For one dreadful moment Biggles thought that the Lovitznian had been joined by his companions, but squirming over on to his back he looked up, and the problem was explained. There were two machines. The fighter, in front and diving steeply, was being closely pursued by a second machine which he recognized instantly. It was the new two-seater which they had captured the previous day. In a flash he understood. He realized that Algy, for some reason not apparent, was not flying the big machine, but that he had to come to look for them in the smaller one. The guns of both machines were going, the Lovitznian aiming at the ditch and the front guns of the two-seater blazing at the machine ahead of it.

This state of affairs did not, however, persist for many seconds, for even if the Lovitznian machine was not being hit, the pilot could not for long remain in ignorance of the fact that he was being attacked. The realization of this must have been as great a shock to him as the appearance of the second machine was to Biggles, but he acted like lightning. In a split second the single-seater was screaming vertically skyward, with the other machine hanging to its tail as if a tow-line connected them.

By this time the others had also realized that something unexpected had happened, and they all stood up in their uncomfortable refuge to watch, spellbound, the end of the affair.

Whether the Lovitznian machine had been hit or not they had no means of knowing; it seemed unlikely that it could have escaped scatheless, yet it showed no signs of being disabled. At the top of the zoom the pilot pulled right over on to his back, and then cleverly flicked a half roll to even keel. In this position he had, of course, a very definite advantage over the larger machine on account of his superior height, for the two-seater had not been able to hold the rocket zoom as long as the smaller machine, but he employed this advantage in a rather surprising manner. Instead of attacking his opponent he whirled round and, putting his nose down for maximum speed, roared away in the direction of the hills, over which he swiftly disappeared. Algy started to follow, but Biggles at once leapt into the open, waving furiously a rather dirty handkerchief.

'If he crosses those hills he's sunk,' he snapped. 'He'll run into the rest of the pack. 'That cunning devil is trying to lead him into a trap. Ah, thank goodness he's got the sense to turn back.'

The two-seater had, in fact, turned, and was now

beginning to circle preparatory to landing. Biggles continued to wave, and by every indication he could think of endeavoured to convey the information that the field was safe to land on. Nevertheless, he could well understand Algy's hesitation, for although the snow was fast disappearing, a thin covering still remained, and there was nothing to show a pilot what lay underneath it.

Biggles stopped waving as the noise of the two-seater's engine died away, and its nose dipped as it glided down to land. They all began to run to the point where it would finish its run.

'Stay where you are,' shouted Biggles to Algy, who was climbing out of his seat as if he intended leaving the machine.

'Why?' asked Algy, pushing up his goggles.

'There are half a dozen more fighters hanging about somewhere. I fancy the fellow you had a go with has gone to fetch them.'

'Is that so?' exclaimed Algy, dropping back into his seat.

'There's no time to talk now,' went on Biggles swiftly. 'You get the Count home as fast as you can and then come back for us.' Biggles turned to the Count. 'In you go, sir. You'd be wise to sit on the floor,' he advised, 'or you may get frost-bitten.'

'I don't like the idea of leaving you here,' protested the Count.

'Don't waste time arguing, please,' said Biggles. 'Seconds are valuable. It's far more important that you should get back. We shan't be long after you, anyway.'

The Count climbed up into the open cockpit and Biggles gave Algy the signal to take off. 'We'll wait for you here,' he shouted, as he backed away.

Algy said nothing. He raised his left hand in a parting

140

salute. The engine roared, and Biggles grabbed a wing-tip to help him to turn. There was no wind, so the direction of the take-off was immaterial* and in a moment the machine was racing, tail up, over the snow, while those on the ground turned their backs to the biting slipstream. They turned again as the machine zoomed into the air, and watched it bank on its course for home. Satisfied that all was well, Biggles then turned towards the farm-house, where several curious spectators were watching.

They had just reached the stable yard when six Lovitznian fighters roared into sight over the hills. Biggles grabbed Ginger by the arm and dragged him into the shelter of a barn, from where they watched the enemy aircraft anxiously.

'Algy only just got away in time,' muttered Biggles. 'I don't think there is anything to worry about now. These fellows will hardly have the nerve to chase one of our machines right across Maltovia.'

'One of *our* machines?' queried Ginger.

'Well, it was carrying Maltovian markings,' smiled Biggles. 'Smyth and Carter have evidently been busy. Ah! There they go,' he added quickly, as the Lovitznian machines turned back towards the hills. 'Good! I shall feel happier with them out of the way. Come on, let us see if we can beg a crust of bread.'

He led the way to the veranda where the owner of the house was standing with his wife and several small children. They had some difficulty in making it understood that they were friends and not enemies, but once this was achieved – chiefly by the production of a Maltovian ten-mark note – a pot of tea, eggs, and a dish of bacon were soon forthcoming.

* Usually an aircraft will take off or land into the wind.

'Algy will have to make two more journeys to get us both back, won't he?' asked Ginger, mopping up bacon fat from the dish with a crust of bread.

'I've been thinking about that,' answered Biggles. 'I don't think so. You and Algy are both fairly light. If fly the machine you should both be able to get in the back seat. It will be a bit of a squeeze, but the machine can carry us all without any difficulty if we can get in.'

The farmer and his family were staring at them wonderingly, which was not surprising, but as there were no means of making them understand the situation, Biggles could not satisfy their curiosity. The meal finished, he just had time to smoke a cigarette before the two-seater was heard returning.

'Make sure it's Algy,' said Ginger cautiously.

'Yes, it's him all right,' replied Biggles, as he saw the machine swing round to land, so after thanking their host as well as they were able to, they hurried back to the field.

It was a tight fit to get two persons into the back seat, but by Ginger lying at full length on the floor, with his legs under the seat, and Algy standing up, it could just be managed. He was, of course, in flying-kit, so the cold would not be likely to trouble him unduly.

Biggles swung himself up into the pilot's seat. His hand closed over the throttle; the engine roared as the machine swung round and, a moment later, was speeding across the snow-covered turf. He did not attempt to climb to any altitude, but at a few hundred feet he levelled out and raced straight back for the aerodrome. There were many things to attend to, and he was anxious to speak to the Count. In twenty minutes by the watch on the instrument board the aerodrome came into view, and it was with real satisfaction that he landed and taxied up the runway into the wood.

'Where the dickens is Smyth?' he growled, as he jumped down and Algy joined him. 'It is not like him to be absent when he is wanted.'

His voice died away curiously as several Maltovian soldiers ran out from the trees. 'What the dickens is all this about, I wonder?' he went on quickly, a suspicion of alarm in his voice. He swung round on his heels as a voice addressed him from behind. An officer stood there, and he was covering them with a revolver. Biggles recognized him at once. It was the thin-lipped aide-de-camp who, with Menkhoff, had accompanied General Bethstein when he had called on them at their hotel. His name, he had learned subsequently, was Vilmsky.

'What is the meaning of this?' Biggles was really angry.

'You are under arrest,' replied Vilmsky suavely.

'By whose orders?'

'General Bethstein's.'

'On what charge?'

'Espionage.'

Biggles nodded slowly. 'So that's the game, is it?' he said softly.

Chapter 16

To Die at Dawn

'It is my duty to warn you that in the event of resistance my orders are to shoot,' went on Vilmsky imperturbably.

'Is that so? I trust you are always as mindful of your duty,' sneered Biggles.

The other scowled but said nothing.

'By what authority does General Bethstein issue such an order as this?' asked Biggles coldly. His object was really to gain time, for he saw that they were in a tight corner, and his brain was feverishly seeking a way out.

'His own,' replied Vilmsky bluntly. 'Where is Lieutenant Hebblethwaite?'

Until that moment Biggles had almost forgotten Ginger; or rather, perhaps, it would be more correct to say that he imagined that he was standing somewhere behind him. He now realized, however, that he must be still lying on the floor of the machine. 'How do you suppose I know?' was his reply to Vilmsky's question. 'You saw us land, didn't you?'

'He isn't here. Where is he?'

'I shouldn't be likely to tell you if I knew.'

'Very well. No doubt we shall find him. Come.'

'Where to?'

'Where we are going to take you.'

'Where is that?'

'To the barracks.'

'Also by the general's orders?'

'You are now under my orders.'

Biggles shrugged his shoulders. He perceived that either resistance or argument was futile, and that the wisest plan was to get away as quickly as possible in order to give Ginger a chance to do something. 'All right,' he said loudly, hoping that Ginger would hear him and take the hint. 'When her Highness hears of this you'll get some orders, my friend – marching orders. How do we travel?'

'My car is waiting.'

'Then let us get on with it. I am very tired and rather cold, so the sooner this nonsense ends, the better.'

Vilmsky snapped an order, and the soldiers lined up on either side of the prisoners.

Algy moved nearer to Biggles. He was white with fury. 'If ever I get my hands on this skunk, or his crooked pal Bethstein, I'll twist their windpipes into a knot that will take a bit of untying,' he breathed vindictively.

Biggles nodded. 'I should have anticipated something of this sort,' he said bitterly, as the party began to move towards the road. 'But to tell the honest truth I did not think that Bethstein would dare to go as far as this. The question is, how far will he go? If he is prepared to go to these lengths to get rid of us he may go to any lengths. Well, we can only wait and see. If we start a rough house they'll shoot us, and there are too many of them for us to hope to get away with it. I have a feeling that Vilmsky would like us to try to get away. I hope they don't separate us, that's all.'

Two cars were waiting on the road. The prisoners, with an escort, were put into the first one and the remainder of the soldiers filled the other. Another order from Vilmsky and the cars began their journey.

'The barracks are somewhere on the other side of the

city,' whispered Algy. 'If they take us right through the main street we may get a chance to do something.'

'They won't,' replied Biggles grimly.

In this assumption he was correct, for soon afterwards the cars took a turning to the right and then proceeded to make a detour round the city. Consequently, it was a good hour before they arrived at their destination, the so-called barracks. The building was, in fact, a medieval fortress modernized in a half-hearted way. The massive gates were closed, but a hoot from the horn brought out a sentry who opened them to admit the cars and then closed them again.

'This place looks more like a jail than a barracks,' muttered Algy, eyeing the old stone walls with disfavour.

'I imagine it would be as hard to break out of,' answered Biggles moodily, as the cars came to a halt in a flagged courtyard, where they were invited to dismount.

No further information was given them as they were marched through a gloomy archway and along a damp corridor, in which their footsteps, and those of their escort, echoed eerily, to what was, without doubt, a cell. The roof was circular, after the manner of a large culvert, and the stone walls were bare of decoration except for countless initials that had been carved on them, apparently by previous prisoners. One of these, with a ghastly sense of humour, had sketched, in charcoal, a grinning skull and crossbones over his monogram. A plain deal table occupied the centre of the floor; a rough wooden form stood beside it, while two crude trestle beds at either end of the apartment completed the furniture. A wan grey light filtered through an iron-barred window high up in the end wall.

'Very pretty,' remarked Algy, with bitter sarcasm, as the door slammed and he stood regarding the skull and crossbones device. 'This place has an unpleasant resemblance to a well-used condemned cell.'

'Try thinking of something cheerful,' suggested Biggles, sitting down on the form and yawning. 'I'm too tired to think.'

'You had an exciting night, I gather?'

'We certainly did,' Biggles told him wearily, and thereafter ran briefly over their adventures for his benefit.

'You didn't expect to find me still in the field when you got back to it, I hope?' said Algy, when he had finished.

'Of course not. You couldn't have done anything, if you had stayed. You were quite right to go home.'

'I waited as long as I dared, but when the snow began to come down good and proper, I decided that my best plan was to get back while I could. I could have come back if the weather had cleared. It was as black as the pit by the time I got home, and but for Smyth's flares I should never have found the aerodrome. As it was, I ran into the trees and smashed a wing-tip. That's why I came over in the two-seater this morning.'

Biggles nodded. 'I thought something of the sort must have happened.'

'As a matter of fact, I had been beetling up and down for the best part of half an hour when I saw that bloke who sports the pennants behaving as though he was shooting up somebody on the ground; I guessed who it was, and down I came in a hurry. He really showed me where you were, because, naturally, I was concentrating on the other side of the river.'

'We saw you,' Biggles told him, 'but we didn't know it was you. You were very high up, and in any case we were expecting the big machine. By the way, what did you do with the Count?'

'I unloaded him at the aerodrome. He insisted that I

should go back for you immediately. The last I saw of him he was walking up the road towards the city. He waved to me as I took off again.'

'I hope he got to the palace all right,' said Biggles quietly. He glanced round suspiciously and dropped his voice to a whisper. 'Ginger is bound to try to get in touch with him, to let him know what has happened. It was a bit of luck for us that he did not get out of the machine. Frankly, had he been caught with us and brought here I wouldn't give a fig for our chance, but if he manages to get clear he will be certain to make a bee-line for the Count, or Ludwig.'

'Even so, they may have a job to find us.'

'I realize that, but they will be certain to guess that Bethstein was at the bottom of it, and they ought to be able to find him even if they don't find us.'

'On the other hand, the cunning devil may take care that they do not,' returned Algy morosely. 'After all, it isn't a bona fide case of arrest on suspicion of espionage. The whole thing is a frame-up arranged by Bethstein to keep us out of the way while he gets on with his dirty work.'

'That is so,' agreed Biggles. 'There was never any doubt about that.'

Further conversation was cut short by the arrival of four guards, armed with rifles with bayonets fixed, under the command of Vilmsky. Biggles stood up and faced them with some surprise, for he had hardly expected them back so soon. He stood still, and advised Algy to do the same, while they were searched, for he realized that resistance was useless. Everything in their pockets having been removed, he turned to Vilmsky expectantly.

'March!' was the curt command.

'What's the idea?' asked Biggles coldly.

148

'You are going to be tried by a military court on a charge of espionage.'

'Espionage my foot,' snapped Biggles. 'Of whom does this court consist?'

'Officers of the Maltovian army.'

Biggles looked at Algy and raised a shoulder helplessly. 'Well, I suppose we'd better go,' he said quietly. 'It's no use fighting and being hauled up by brute force like a couple of pickpockets.' He turned to Vilmsky, who was regarding them with a supercilious smile. 'Lead on,' he said grimly.

Back along the corridor they marched and then up a flight of stone stairs that emerged on to a wide landing. Outside a door two sentries were on duty. They stood aside when they saw the prisoners and their escort. Vilmsky opened the door and walked in. Unhurriedly, with Algy close behind, Biggles followed, his eyes taking in the scene.

Within the room, a lofty chamber lighted by several lamps, for the winter afternoon was drawing in, five men were sitting behind a long refectory table. All wore the uniforms and badges of rank of senior officers of the Maltovian army. On the table, which was covered by a green baize cloth, were sheets of paper and writing materials. That was all.

All eyes were on the prisoners as they advanced slowly towards the table, but Biggles's hostile gaze was fixed on one man, obviously the president of the court, for he sat at the centre of the table with two others on either side. It was General Bethstein.

The general returned his stare. 'Is your name Bigglesworth?' he asked in a loud voice.

Biggles's lips curled slightly. 'Why waste time asking fool questions?' he said harshly. 'You know it is.'

'Answer my question!'

'Let me ask you one. What is the meaning of this farce?'

The general leaned forward. 'You do not appear to realize that you are being tried on a charge for which, if you are found guilty, the punishment is death,' he said evenly.

'And you, having found us guilty before the trial begins, are only waiting to pass sentence. Am I right?'

The general's eyes half closed. 'Insolence will not help your case,' he grated.

'Neither will anything else, I imagine.'

'Silence!'

Biggles regarded the other members of the court in turn. There was not a single friendly face among them – not that he expected to find one, knowing that they must all be fellow conspirators of the general's or they would not be there. He turned back to Bethstein. 'Who are all these people?' he asked, indicating the court.

'They are officcrs of the Maltovian army.'

'Friends of yours, I presume?'

The general eyed him malevolently. 'It would seem that you do not take these proceedings seriously,' he said in a hard voice.

'On the contrary, I take them very seriously indeed,' answered Biggles evenly.

'Very well. Let us proceed.' The general cleared his throat. 'What is your nationality?'

'That is something else you know, but you are likely to know a thundering sight better if you try any monkey tricks and the British Foreign Office gets to hear of it, as it certainly will.'

'Will you answer the questions put to you?' snapped the general, who was obviously fast losing his temper.

'No, I won't,' returned Biggles tersely. 'This court is irregular, and you know it. You have no right to detain us, much less hold this farcical trial. I know what you are doing as well as you do, and as well as every one else in the room knows, no doubt. Why waste time with these absurd proceedings? If you fondly imagine that they will save your face you are making a big mistake, so cut out the nonsense and do what you have already decided to do.'

The general smiled curiously and picked up his pen. 'No one shall say that you did not have a fair trial,' he said mockingly. 'Where were you last night?'

'You evidently know that, or you wouldn't ask.'

'Were you in Lovitzna?'

'I was.'

The general wrote something on the paper in front of him and then looked at the other members of the court triumphantly. 'You heard that?' he said sharply. 'The prisoner admits he was in Lovitzna.'

An idea suddenly occurred to Biggles. Somehow – he did not know how – the general had learned of their visit to the enemy country. Did he know the reason, he wondered? 'Do you know why I went to Lovitzna last night?' he inquired.

The general started, making it clear that he did not. 'Why did you go?' he asked in an odd tone of voice.

Biggles noted that the atmosphere of the room had suddenly become tense. 'I went to fetch somebody,' he said quietly, looking the general straight in the eyes. 'Can you guess who it was?'

Suspicion, and then understanding, flashed across the general's face. 'So,' he ejaculated in a voice that trembled with rage.

'So,' mimicked Biggles. 'I am pleased to be able to inform you that you went to a lot of trouble for nothing, although as a loyal subject of Maltovia you should be delighted to learn that Count Stanhauser is now at the palace. I and my friends brought him home, and that, I think, knocks on the head once and for all any charge of espionage. I'll bet you don't write *that* down on your paper.'

The general's lips came together in an ominous line. 'You lie,' he snarled.

Biggles's eyes flashed as his temper got out of control. 'You call me a liar? If there is a liar in this room it is you, you dirty, yellow, double-crossing spy.'

The general sprang to his feet livid with fury. In his convulsive grip the pen he held in his hand broke across the middle. He flung the pieces on the table and reached for his revolver, but he checked himself in time. 'I think we have heard enough,' he almost hissed.

'I thought you'd soon get tired of hearing the truth,' sneered Biggles.

The general turned to the court. 'What is your verdict, gentlemen?' he asked.

'Guilty,' came the answer, as in a single voice.

The general drew a deep breath and sat down heavily. 'You heard that?' He glowered at the prisoners. 'It now falls to me to pronounce sentence.'

'Pah! Don't waste your breath.' Biggles's voice was heavy with loathing and disgust.

The general stood up, smiling sardonically. 'The sentence of this court is that you be taken to the place from whence you came, and at the break of dawn be shot to death by a party of soldiers detailed for that purpose.'

'You must have recited that little piece a good many times to bring it out as pat as that,' jeered Biggles.

'And may God have mercy on your soul,' concluded the general piously.

'Save your good wishes for yourself. You'll need them,' taunted Biggles.

A heavy hand fell on his arm and swung him round. The escort closed in around them and marched them back to their cell. The door closed with a dull clang. A key grated in the lock.

Biggles looked at Algy with a whimsical smile on his face. 'The biggest blunder I ever made in my life was to underestimate that scoundrel's villainy,' he said bitterly.

'You think he means it?'

Biggles sat down on the table and thrust his hands into his pockets. 'My dear fellow,' he said quietly, 'we have been in several awkward corners in our long and somewhat chequered careers, but never in such a tight one as this.'

'What are we going to do about it?'

Biggles glanced round the bare stone walls. 'There doesn't seem to be much we can do, does there?' he said coolly.

Chapter 17

Ginger Takes the Warpath

Ginger, lying on the bottom of the fuselage of the two-seater at the moment when the arrest was made, nearly gave himself away by his impetuosity, although it is true that he had no reason to suspect that matters were as serious as they really were. The actual sequence of events occurred in this order.

After Algy had got out of the cockpit, he, Ginger, at once moved to follow him, but found to his annoyance that owing to his cramped position his right leg had what is called 'gone to sleep'. Muttering in his impatience, he proceeded to massage it vigorously to restore the circulation, and he was still employed in this unusual occupation when a few words of a conversation reached his ears, words that caused him to cease rubbing and adopt a curious attitude of attention. The actual words he heard were Biggles's sharply uttered 'What is the meaning of this?' when he had found himself suddenly confronted by Vilmsky. Needless to say he listened – all ears, as the saying is – for the reply, and he started when he heard Vilmsky's suave 'You are under arrest.'

His next action was purely instinctive. Naturally, he wanted to see what was going on. Grabbing the seat, he pulled himself up, and for two or three seconds gazed wonderingly at the scene below him. It was fortunate for him, although in the circumstances it was only natural, that all eyes were on Biggles and Algy, for which reason his jack-in-the-box appearance passed unobserved. If, at that moment, he had made the slightest sound, or had one of the soldiers looked in his direction, he would, inevitably, have been discovered. Upon such slender threads do lives sometimes hang. Once the realization of what was happening penetrated into his startled brain, he sank down again, and from the floor of the cockpit heard the rest of the conversation.

The few minutes' duration of this saw him in a fever of indecision, for without warning he found himself faced by a major problem. Two courses were open to him. Either he could sit still in the hope of escaping, when subsequently he might be able to effect a rescue, or he could attempt a rescue there and then. He had a loaded pistol in his pocket. Could he, with any real hope of success, take on seven or eight men – for he had seen at least that number – armed with rifles? No, he decided, he could not. In the fracas that would certainly ensue, it was inconceivable that none of them would be shot, and thus, instead of averting a tragedy, he might be the means of causing one. In the end he decided on the former plan, although he drew his pistol prepared to put the latter into execution if discovery became imminent. As it happened, no one thought of looking into the two-seater from which two men had already emerged.

He not only heard the rest of the affair, but he saw it, through a tiny hole which he cut in the fabric of the fuselage with the point of his pen-knife. He watched Biggles and Algy being marched across to the cars, and saw the cars disappear up the road in the direction of Janovica. Then, and not before, did he risk a cautious peep over the rim of the cockpit. Not a soul was in sight. Silence reigned. Where was Smyth? And Carter? Surely they should be about, or had they been arrested, too?

155

Stealthily, with his pistol gripped ready for use, he climbed over the edge of the cockpit and dropped lightly to the ground. He could still see no one, so he darted into the trees and from there made a careful survey of the temporary hangar. Still he saw no one. Slowly, with every nerve taut, he crept forward until he stood at last at the entrance of the hangar. As his eyes probed the dim interior he saw Smyth, tied hand and foot, a bandage over his mouth, strapped to one of the upright logs. Ginger started to run towards him, but pulled up with a jerk as his horror-stricken eyes fell on something else. Carter lay at full length on the floor with his face in a little pool of blood.

With trembling fingers Ginger took out his pen-knife and, not without difficulty, managed to get Smyth free. The sergeant almost collapsed when he attempted to move. 'Look after Carter; I'm all right,' he said weakly. 'What about the Skipper, and Mr Lacey?'

'They've got them,' Ginger told him bitterly. 'What happened here?'

'They just rushed in on us before we had a chance to do anything,' answered Smyth, dropping on his knees beside his comrade.

'Is he dead?' asked Ginger breathlessly.

'I don't think so. He started scrapping, and a dirty skunk knocked him on the head with a rifle-butt.'

'I'll do some knocking on the head before I'm through with this bunch of thugs,' swore Ginger. 'Look, sergeant. I shall have to leave you here to take care of Carter while I go and let the Count or Mr Ludwig Stanhauser know what has happened. I'll have a doctor sent down to you if I can.'

'You get off, sir. I'll manage somehow,' Smyth told him. 'Try to let me know what happens.'

'I will,' Ginger promised, and putting the pistol in his pocket, he set off at a run towards the road. In fact, he ran all the way to the hotel, where he arrived breathless and nearly exhausted. Josef, who was sitting at his little desk, hurried towards him with concern written on his face when he saw the state his guest was in.

'Vot iss it?' he asked tremulously.

Ginger swallowed hard. 'Try to get Lieutenant Stanhauser on the telephone, will you?' he gasped. 'I must speak to him, or to Count Stanhauser, at once.'

Josef fetched him something in a glass and then disappeared into his office. When he returned a few minutes later Ginger was more normal.

'Well?' he inquired breathlessly.

'The lieutenant, he comes,' declared Josef. 'By good chance he wos at 'ome.'

Ginger sat down with a deep sigh of relief, while Josef hurried away and returned presently with some cold food on a plate, which Ginger attacked ravenously for he had not realized how hungry he was. He was also very tired, but the food helped to restore him. He pushed the plate aside, however, and sprang to his feet as Ludwig burst into the room. His face was pale with anxiety.

'What has happened?' he asked tensely.

In as few words as possible, Ginger told him.

'But this is absurd. The general would not dare to do such a thing,' declared Ludwig.

'Wouldn't he? He's done it,' answered Ginger, pacing up and down.

'And you heard Vilmsky say they were going to the barracks?'

'That's what he said.'

'I will send a doctor to your mechanic at once, then I will see the Count. He is at the palace. If your friends are in the barracks we will soon have them out, don't worry. Remain here. Do nothing. I will come back.'

Ginger caught Ludwig by the arm as he was hurrying from the room. 'Don't you let the Count go to the barracks by himself,' he warned him. 'There is no knowing what Bethstein will do. He is engineering something, and it must be pretty near zero hour for that to happen, whatever it may be, or he wouldn't risk such high-handed action as arresting Biggles.'

'Do not fear. I shall not be long,' said Ludwig confidently.

In this, however, he was mistaken, for darkness had fallen and the lamps had been lighted before he returned.

Ginger, who had spent the hours feverishly pacing the room took one look at his face and felt his heart sink. 'Well?' he asked.

'They cannot be found,' said Ludwig wearily.

Ginger sank into a chair. 'Cannot be found?' he echoed foolishly.

'We have tried everywhere.'

'But I distinctly heard Vilmsky say they were going to the barracks.'

'Major Berner, one of her Highness's Imperial Guards, has been there. He says that the officer in charge of the garrison denies all knowledge of any English prisoners.'

'Rot! I don't believe it,' stormed Ginger. 'Bethstein has got them locked up there. What has he got to say about it, anyway?'

'We have been unable to find him.'

Ginger stared incredulously. 'Do you mean to tell me that in a country which calls itself civilized, on the eve of war, the government cannot get into touch with the commander-in-chief of its army?'

Ludwig shrugged his shoulders. 'We only know that he

is indisposed and has gone into the country for a short rest.'

'He'll have a long rest if I ever get him where I want him,' grated Ginger, white-faced. 'Such a rest that he'll never wake up again. Well, what are we going to do about it?'

'Can you suggest anything? Her Highness and the Count are prepared to do anything, but they have already done all in their power. They cannot order your friends' release until they know where they are and who is holding them.'

'No, I suppose that's true enough,' agreed Ginger disconsolately. 'Would it be any use my seeing the Count?'

'He will see you with pleasure if you think it will help matters, but I think you should realize that the government is working feverishly to save the situation.'

'What situation?'

'War. Things are fast coming to a head. We can feel it in the air. The soldiers know it. You can see it on the faces of the people. Bethstein has engineered a *coup d'état**, there is no doubt of that, and the storm may break at any moment.'

'What will happen if it does?'

'The princess may have to fly from the country.'

'Good heavens! Is it as bad as that?'

'Unhappily, yes. You and your friends have done much, and I believe it is fear of what you may yet do that caused Bethstein to hasten his plans. In the circumstances, individuals must take second place to affairs of state, and you must forgive the princess and the Count if they do not devote their whole time to your friends, much as they

---

* French expression meaning a violent and illegal attempt to seize control of a country.

would like to help them and anxious as they are for their safety.'

'Yes, I appreciate that,' replied Ginger slowly. 'Perhaps it would be better if I kept out of the way. What is the government doing about all this?'

'It is busy making plans on the lines suggested by your chief, but I am afraid we have left it rather late and it is now a race against time.'

Ginger nodded. As far as he was concerned the affairs of Maltovia were now of secondary importance. 'What are you going to do?' he asked.

'For the moment I am at your disposal, but when Bethstein strikes I shall have to leave you and go to my regiment. You understand that if Bethstein succeeds in his plan, loyal people like myself will lose their lives.'

'And I shall lose mine, or Bethstein his,' declared Ginger savagely. 'He's the man I'm going to find. You say he has gone into the country? Where would that be likely to be?'

'I expect he would go to his hunting-box.'

Ginger started. 'Why, that's the place that was marked on the map we found in the Lovitznian aeroplane.'

'Yes, that is so.'

Ginger struck the table with his fist. 'That's it!' he cried. 'That is where the plot is hatching. How far away is it?'

'Forty miles – perhaps a little more.'

'You've got a car?'

'Yes.'

'Where is it?'

'Outside.'

'Come on, then, let's go.'

Ludwig hesitated. 'It's rather a risky thing to do, isn't it, like – how do you say? – jumping into the lion's mouth?'

Ginger smiled cynically. 'Ludwig,' he said frankly, 'if

160

you people had tackled the lion a little earlier, you wouldn't be in the mess you are in now. Well, I'm going to jump into Bethstein's den with a pistol in my hand. It's time he was shown a thing or two. The question is, do I go by myself or are you coming with me?'

A curious gleam came into Ludwig's eyes. 'I believe you're right,' he said. 'I will come with you.'

'Got a pistol?'

'Yes.'

'That's fine. Then let's get a move on.' Ginger looked at the clock. 'Seven o'clock. We ought to be there before nine.'

'I must report to the Count before I go.'

'All right. You can tell him to stand by for a big bang. I've got a feeling in my bones that I am going to make a noise before this night is over.'

Ludwig smiled. 'I'll help you do it,' he promised enthusiastically. 'Things have been quiet here for too long.'

'Much too long,' agreed Ginger.

Chapter 18

A Startling Discovery

Ginger had never been so worried in his life as he was during the run out to the general's hunting-box, which was situated in the midst of wild, uncultivated country, for now that he had taken the plunge a doubt had arisen in his mind, and he could not shake off the feeling that he might be running away from Biggles instead of towards him. Moreover, it was a good deal later than he had estimated, for Ludwig had been detained for some time at the palace. Of the conversation that had taken place between the Count and his nephew he knew nothing beyond the fact that the Count had said that he could not see what good purpose they hoped to serve by leaving Janovica. So much Ludwig had admitted. Nor, for that matter, could Ginger. He had made no plans, nor did he know what he hoped to achieve beyond the wild idea that if he could get within striking distance of the general he would force him, by violence if necessary, to tell him where Biggles and Algy were being detained. Had he known the true facts of the case, that they were, at that moment, lying under sentence of death, anything might have happened, so perhaps it was as well that he did not. As it was, he had calmed somewhat by the time Ludwig, who was driving, slowed down and declared that they were getting near their destination.

'How far are we away from the house itself?' asked Ginger.

'About a mile,' was the answer. 'It lies about half a mile back from the road. The estate is a big one; this is all part of it.' Ludwig indicated the sombre fir forest through which they were passing.

'I see; go steady,' ordered Ginger, who had more or less taken charge of the expedition. 'It's no use barging right up to the front door.'

Ludwig stopped the car by the side of the road. 'What are we going to do now we are here?' he asked.

'I've been thinking,' replied Ginger. 'I believe the best plan would be for you to crawl along now until we find an opening in the trees where we can put the car out of sight in case any one comes along. With the lights out it is unlikely that it would be seen. You stay with the car while I go off and have a scout round and get the lie of the land. I may be able to learn something. If I don't come back in, say, a couple of hours, you'll know that I am a prisoner, too, but you will at least know where I am. If that happens, you will have to please yourself what you do about it.'

Ludwig demurred. 'Surely it would be better if I came with you,' he protested.

Ginger shook his head. 'No,' he said conclusively. 'Quite apart from any other consideration, it wouldn't do for you to be caught prowling around the general's establishment like a burglar. You are an important person in Maltovia. It doesn't matter two hoots about me.'

'Very well, if you think it is better that way.'

'Good! Then that's settled,' murmured Ginger. 'Here's an opening – yes, this will do; it's the very place,' he went on quickly, as they came to a narrow glade in the trees. 'You park yourself and the car in there and wait. Don't get jumpy and shoot me by mistake when I come back. I'll give a low whistle to let you know it's me.'

'Yes, it should be safe here,' agreed Ludwig. 'You'll find the entrance to the drive about a quarter of a mile along, on the right-hand side of the road.'

'I'll find it,' said Ginger confidently, and, keeping on the grass edge that bordered the road, he set off at a steady trot towards his objective.

He slowed down, however, before he had gone very far, and began to scout the ground ahead carefully before he ventured on to it, for he was quite prepared to find guards posted. There were, in fact, two men standing at the entrance to the drive, although whether they were guards he did not know, for he did not venture close enough to them to see if they wore uniforms. He heard them talking some time before they came into sight, but once he had located their position he had no difficulty in avoiding them by making a detour through the trees, which brought him to the drive some distance inside the gates.

He surveyed the ground carefully before leaving the heavy shadow of the trees. In the light of the moon, which had now risen, from the point where he stood he saw that the drive ran as straight as a ruled line across an open field, or park, of considerable extent, this being bounded on three sides by the forest. At the far end lay the house, or hunting-box, its exact position made clear by two lighted windows, and towards this he now started to make his way, taking care to keep in shadow. It was as well that he took this precaution, for at the next aspect, presented by a curve in the edge of the wood, he saw something that excited his curiosity.

Some fifty or sixty yards from the edge of the forest – that is to say, in the open meadow – a man was standing near a small dark object which lay on the grass. So still did he stand that he might have been a statue, and as he continued to creep along the fringe of the forest Ginger often stopped to stare wonderingly. Had the fellow carried a rifle he might have been a sentry, he thought, but even so, it was an odd place to take up a position, and most sentries marched to and fro on a regular beat – at least, so he had always understood.

The mystery was still unsolved when he reached a shrubbery that formed a boundary to the gardens round the house, and through this he attempted to force a path; but in the dense shadow of the evergreens it was inky black, and after nearly losing an eye on the stump of a branch, he desisted, and decided to find a way round. It was nervy work, for it was impossible to move without making some slight noise, and every moment he expected to hear a challenge ring out. Nothing of the sort happened, however, and he reached the badly kept flower beds inside the shrubbery without incident, apart from nearly falling into a lily-pond, the dark water of which he mistook for a shadow.

He was now standing within a dozen paces of the front of the house, a fairly large modern brick building with a good deal of ornate decoration. A creeper-covered porch protruded from the centre and hid the actual doorway from view. There were several windows on either side of it and behind two of these lights were burning, one at either end of the house. So bright were these lights that he stared at them for some time trying to make out what was unusual about them apart from the blinds not being drawn, which in itself struck him as strange. Creeping towards the larger of the two, which was the one on the left-hand side of the porch, suddenly he understood. A powerful lamp had been so placed just inside the room that its beams were directed through the window, and threw an orange path of light across the overgrown lawn.

This discovery only mystified him still more, and he was just thinking of going nearer when, without warning, the front door was thrown open and two men stepped outside.

Ginger, with his heart in his mouth, as the saying is, shrank back into the shrubbery, but he did not take his eyes from the two men. One he recognized at once. It was General Bethstein. The other, a short, rather fat, middle-aged man with a large nose and no hair on the front of his head, was a stranger, and he wondered whom he could be until he caught the word 'Klein' at the termination of something the general had said. Then he knew that he was looking at the banker of whom Ludwig had spoken when they had had the discussion at the hotel. Of what they were talking about he did not know, for the conversation was conducted in a language unknown to him, although he assumed that it was Maltovian.

For a few minutes the men stood on the step, looking up at the sky as though they were discussing the weather. Then Bethstein looked at his watch, and said something in an undertone, after which they both went back into the house.

Ginger breathed again, not knowing whether to be pleased or angry that they had gone. His first impulse had been to draw his pistol and rush out, demanding of the general the whereabouts of his friends, but something made him shrink from this course. Or perhaps it would be better to say that the odd circumstance of the lighted windows suggested to him that if he remained quiet he might make an important discovery.

Within a very few minutes he knew that his decision had been the right one, and the first intimation of it came when an unmistakable sound reached his ears. It was the faraway drone of an aero engine. It persisted only for a short time and then died away abruptly, so abruptly that he knew that the throttle had been retarded. In a flash he understood everything, the meaning of the lighted windows and the interest of Bethstein and Klein in the sky. And when, a moment later, three lights glowed in different corners of the park, the mystery of the solitary man was explained. He had been waiting to signal to the aircraft.

Ginger was now trembling with excitement. He remembered Biggles's casual remark about the marked area on the map, and its connection with the leakage of information. He knew now that he had been right, and that aeroplanes were going to and fro between the general's retreat and Lovitzna. No wonder the traitor was in close touch with the enemy, thought Ginger bitterly. He now had to decide what was the best course of action, and it involved some weighty consideration, but in the end he decided to wait and see what happened before moving. Listening intently, he soon heard the faint hum of the gliding aeroplane, and shortly afterwards the peculiar noise made by shock absorbers when the wheels of an aeroplane are running over rough ground. The front door was thrown open again, and Bethstein and Klein reappeared, evidently to meet their visitor. He was not long arriving, and so close did he pass to Ginger's hiding-place that he covered his face with his arms, fearing that he might be seen. But as soon as the man had gone past he looked up, and the light from the illuminated window shone on the face of the new arrival. He drew in his breath sharply as he recognized Zarovitch.

A word of greeting, and the three men disappeared into the house. The door closed quietly and a chain rattled inside it. A few moments later the powerful lamps inside the two windows were switched out, and the house was wrapped in comparative darkness, comparative because a faint yellow glow persisted in the room on the left hand side of the door, suggesting that an ordinary lamp was still burning there.

Ginger darted towards it, taking care to keep below the level of the sill, but if he hoped to watch what went on inside the room – and that was, of course, his object – he was doomed to disappointment. He just had time to see Zarovitch take a sheaf of documents from a portfolio he carried when, with a loud swish, a heavy curtain was drawn across the window completely cutting out his view. For a moment he lingered, torn by indecision. The situation was, he decided, too important and too critical for him to handle alone. He could not afford to risk failure. Turning, he crept back to the shrubbery, and then, after a swift but intense study of the field, he darted to the edge of the forest. Reaching it, he paused for a moment to listen, and then sped back towards the place where he had left Ludwig. He did not relax his vigilance, however, but scouted every turning before he took it. Nor did he forget the prearranged signal. An answering whistle from Ludwig, and he ran forward. During his journey he had been thinking hard, so he had his plan ready.

'Ludwig,' he whispered in a voice of suppressed excitement, 'we have got Bethstein cold. Listen! He is in the house with Klein, the banker, and Zarovitch, the Lovitznian Foreign Minister. Zarovitch has just arrived by air and he has brought a packet of documents with him – for Bethstein to sign, I think. I saw him take the papers out of a case. If he will only stay there long enough we can catch the plotters red-handed, but we can't do it alone. Have you got any troops, or police, whom you can trust implicitly?'

'My own regiment would follow me anywhere, so would the princess's guards.'

'Then go and get them. To be on the safe side, to

surround the house and make sure that no one escapes, we need at least twenty men. Grab some cars and bring them along. Allowing for an hour each way, and a quarter of an hour at the other end, you should be back in just over a couple of hours – say, by half-past two.'

Ginger's eager enthusiasm communicated itself to Ludwig. 'Suppose Zarovitch leaves?' he asked tensely.

'I'll see to it he doesn't get away. If necessary I'll plug the swine and grab the documents. In any case, it is more than likely that Bethstein will have some incriminating evidence about the house. Will you go?'

'Of course.' Ludwig sprang into the driving seat of his car.

'When you come back I should unload the men and park the cars here,' Ginger told him. 'Make a detour round the gate in case any one is on guard. Go straight down the edge of the forest until you come to a shrubbery. If no one has left the house I will be waiting for you there. Speed is the great thing now, but for heaven's sake don't have an accident.'

'I'll do my best,' promised Ludwig, and the car bumped on to the road. An instant later it was racing towards Janovica.

Ginger waited until it was out of earshot, and then, praying that Zarovitch was still there, he made his way swiftly back towards the house.

Chapter 19

Ginger Gets a Prisoner – and a Shock

As he crept down the side of the silent forest he knew that the Lovitznian had not left, for he saw the moonlight glistening on the wings of an aeroplane on the far side of the field. He reached the shrubbery without trouble or alarm, where, finding, as he had expected, that the blinds were still drawn, he made his way along until he came to a spot, some distance from the house – but from where he could watch it – which he thought Zarovitch would have to pass when he returned to the machine. There, in the pitch black shadow of a low-hanging yew, he settled down to wait.

The time passed slowly, so slowly that he lost all count of it. He did not mind. Indeed, it suited him, for he was praying that Zarovitch would remain inside the building until reinforcements arrived. He knew that if the plan had not miscarried it could not now be long before Ludwig returned, and when that time came he would have to go back to the shrubbery to meet him as arranged.

Another quarter of an hour passed, and he was just thinking of moving when he heard the door of the house open and saw a beam of light fall across the lawn. 'Confound it!' he thought. 'He might have stayed a little longer.' Then he crept back still farther into the shadow as he saw a figure walking briskly towards him, and knew from the gait and the portfolio that it was Zarovitch. The door of the house had closed behind the departing conspirator and utter silence reigned.

Ginger's heart began to beat a little faster as he took out his pistol and held it ready. The critical moment had come. He waited until the plotter was within ten yards, then he stepped out in front of him, pistol thrust forward. 'Stand quite still, Zarovitch,' he said quietly. 'The thing in my hand is a pistol. It is loaded. If you so much as make one yelp, or take one step in the wrong direction, I swear on my oath I'll shoot you dead.' There was a ring of sincerity in his voice that could not be mistaken.

Zarovitch did not answer. He stood quite still. Indeed, there was nothing he could do.

Ginger took a pace nearer. 'Turn round and walk,' he ordered. 'And remember as you walk that the muzzle of my pistol is only six inches from your back. Watch your step. You have only to stumble and it will go off.'

'One moment,' said Zarovitch, speaking with an effort as though he was suffering from shock, which no doubt he was. 'What will you take to withdraw and forget this incident?'

'Nothing,' replied Ginger bluntly. 'I don't bargain with crooks. Keep your mouth shut and walk – and don't look back.'

'But—'

'Don't argue. I'm tired, and I'd sooner shoot than talk.'

'Where do we go?'

'You'll see. Get going.'

The Lovitznian turned and began walking, with Ginger following close behind. 'Make for the edge of the forest opposite,' he ordered. 'And now turn to the right,' he continued when they reached it, and in this way they progressed until they reached the road. Down the road they marched, Ginger still covering his prisoner. Inwardly, he was getting more than a little anxious, for he had fully expected to meet Ludwig before this. The time allowed for his return had elapsed, and he began to wonder what he would do with Zarovitch if Ludwig did not return. They reached the clearing in the trees, where Ginger gave the order to halt.

'For what are we waiting here?' asked the Lovitznian.

'You'll see,' Ginger told him, with more confidence than he felt. He was, in fact, becoming thoroughly alarmed by Ludwig's non-appearance, and he began to visualize all sorts of dire calamities.

Shortly afterwards, however, his heart gave a jump when a distant hum of a motor-car engine reached his ears, but he did not really relax until Ludwig's car ran smoothly to a standstill and he saw Ludwig himself step out. Three more cars were following close behind, none of them carrying lights. Ginger stared when Count Stanhauser himself, in general's uniform, got out. 'Here I am, sir, over here,' he said quietly.

'Why – what – good heavens! What is this?' exclaimed the Count, as he saw Ginger and his prisoner standing in the shadow.

'Zarovitch was departing, sir, so I thought I had better detain him,' explained Ginger. 'May I suggest that you examine the contents of his portfolio? I fancy you will find something very interesting in it. And if you will detail two men to take charge of the prisoner, I should be very glad.'

It was Ludwig who ordered an escort for the Lovitznian, for the Count was busy with the contents of the portfolio, which he was already examining with the assistance of a pocket-torch. Zarovitch, silent and glowering, was placed in one of the cars under the muzzles of four rifles, and, thus relieved, Ginger turned to Ludwig.

'You've been a long time,' he said. 'I was afraid something had gone wrong.'

'It took longer than we thought to organize the party,' Ludwig told him. 'The Count had gone home, and cars had to be found. Nerves in the city are very jumpy. Martial law has been proclaimed, and my uncle has taken over control of both the police and military forces. That is why he is in uniform.'

The Count joined them, and they could tell by the gravity of his expression that Ginger's estimate of the contents of the portfolio had not been far wrong.

'Have you found evidence to incriminate General Bethstein, sir?' asked Ludwig.

'Evidence! Incriminate him!' The Count appeared to find difficulty in saying the words. 'That arch-scoundrel would have sold his country to her enemies. The agreement is here, signed and sealed. In return for Bethstein's assistance, Maltovia is to be a dependency of Lovitzna, with Bethstein as Governor-General. His signature, too, is on the deed, which I imagine was just on its way back to Shavros. The signature was what Zarovitch came for, no doubt. Klein is also a party to the plot. It seems that we may just be in time to save the situation. With Bethstein and Klein under lock and key with Zarovitch, and the story of their infamy broadcast to the nation, the whole country will be against them and their plans will come to nothing. But we must not stand talking here.'

'What are you going to do, sir?'

'I am going formally to arrest General Bethstein and Klein on a charge of high treason.' The Count turned to Ginger. 'You had better show us the way,' he said.

'Very good, sir. Get the men in line and tell them to maintain absolute silence.'

A buzz of conversation ran through the troops when the

173

Count told them of the general's defection, and some dark looks were thrown at the Lovitznian sitting under guard in the back of the car. Then order was restored, and in single file, with Ginger at the head, they set off towards the house. As they emerged from the forest he halted and pointed to the aeroplane, still waiting for its passenger. 'How many men have we got, sir?' he asked the Count.

'Twenty, now; we started with twenty-four.'

'Then I suggest that you send two more to arrest the pilot of that aircraft. I don't suppose that Zarovitch flew it over himself. If they keep under cover of the trees they will probably take the pilot by surprise; he has been waiting a long time and is probably getting rather bored.'

The precaution taken, and the two men on their way, the main party resumed its march, and did not halt again until it stood in the shadow of the shrubbery. Ginger crept forward but was soon back.

'The light is still burning in the general's room,' he whispered, 'so presumably he and Klein are still there. The door is chained on the inside, I believe, and they will hardly be likely to open it if they see who is at the door. I think the situation calls for a little strategy, sir. It is not unlikely that they will be wondering why the aircraft has not taken off, and if that is so they would not be very astonished if Zarovitch returned. Could you imitate his voice, sir?'

'Yes, fairly well, I think,' answered the Count.

'Then I suggest that you conceal the men round the door and then go and knock on it. If Bethstein asks who is there, say Zarovitch. When the door is open we will rush it and take the general by surprise before he gets a chance to destroy any incriminating documents.'

'I think that is a good plan,' agreed the Count, and forthwith proceeded with the execution of it. It did not

174

occupy many seconds, and with the men in position, he knocked boldly on the front door.

'There was a brief delay. Then, 'Who is there?' came from the inside.

'It is I – Zarovitch,' replied the Count, in a fair imitation of the Lovitznian's voice.

A chain rattled and the door swung open.

Ginger led the rush and thrust his foot so that the door could not be closed again. 'Just a minute, General Bethstein,' he said evenly. 'There is somebody here to see you.'

'What is the meaning of this?' cried the general, with some agitation as he saw the soldiers. He began to back away.

Ginger whipped out his pistol. 'Stand still both of you,' he said in a hard voice, for he saw Klein standing behind the general.

Count Stanhauser moved forward. 'General Bethstein, you are under arrest,' he said coldly.

'What nonsense is this? Are you mad, Stanhauser?' exclaimed the general hoarsely.

'No. Rather have I come to my senses,' replied the Count calmly. 'I propose to search your study.' He called two soldiers by name and they took up positions on either side of the general. 'Don't move, Klein; I want you, too,' went on the Count.

Ginger whispered something in his ear and he turned back to the general. 'Where is Major Bigglesworth?' he asked tersely.

A faint, peculiar smile flitted across the general's face. 'He is in safe keeping,' he said slowly.

'Where is he?'

'That foreigner has upset my plans,' said the general viciously. 'He will upset no more plans.'

175

Ginger felt his heart go cold. 'What do you mean?' he asked quickly.

The general smiled mockingly. 'At the barracks, before I came here, I had the satisfaction of sentencing him to death,' he said harshly. 'The sentence is to be carried out at dawn.'

The colour drained from Ginger's face. He turned to the Count. 'What is the time?' he asked in a high-pitched voice.

The Count looked at his watch. 'It is now – five o'clock.'

Ginger's brain reeled. He tried to think, but could not. 'What time does the sun rise?' he managed to get out.

'I can tell you that,' put in the general imperturbably. 'It rises at five-thirty.'

'Why, that's in – in – in half an hour,' stammered Ginger, feeling that the ground was rocking under his feet. Odd phrases flashed through his mind. Forty miles – half an hour – forty miles—

'It is impossible to reach the barracks in half an hour,' said the Count, who seemed to be nearly as upset as Ginger. 'It will take you twenty minutes to get to the car, and no car in the world could get to Janovica in half an hour, much less ten minutes. It is forty-three miles.'

Ginger's face was ashen. 'Is there a telephone here?' he cried almost hysterically.

The general shook his head. 'No,' he said, 'there isn't a telephone between here and Janovica.'

Ginger moistened his lips. 'Good heavens!' he whispered. 'What are we going to do?'

Chapter 20

Backs to the Wall

Biggles spent most of the night sitting on the edge of the table. He was deadly tired, but he did not feel inclined to spend in sleep time which might be employed in thinking of some plan of escape. Algy sat on the bench, with his hands in his pockets and his feet on the table. He had examined the door and the walls a hundred times, and was satisfied that nothing short of a charge of dynamite would move them. He had also spent some time at the window, which could be reached by standing on the bench, but the bars were immovable, and even if it had been possible to remove them, the opening would still have been too small to get through.

'No, I'm afraid there's nothing doing,' said Biggles swinging his legs gently. 'This is one of those things which no ordinary man can make allowances for. When you're dealing with a fellow like Bethstein, until you know just how unscrupulous he is, anything can happen. He is the sort of thug who would employ assassins, and even kings with all their guards sometimes fall victims. Admittedly, we've known all along that he was working for the other side – but there, what's the use of talking? We're here, and unless he was putting up a gigantic bluff, which I do not for one moment believe, he will have us put out of the way for good as soon as it gets light enough to see.'

'What is the time now, do you suppose?'

'I haven't the vaguest idea, but if you ask for my opinion I should say it is about five o'clock; my watch has stopped – not that I could see it, anyway.'

'What time does it get light?'

'Somewhere about half-past five.'

'What the dickens is Ginger doing? I should have thought he would have got busy as soon as he saw the jam we were in.'

'We don't know for certain that he got away. Assuming that he did, I imagine he would go and tell Ludwig or the Count what had happened. They would make inquiries, of course, but I doubt if they would rush about all night for the simple reason that they could not possibly imagine our case being so desperate as it is. Bethstein probably realizes that, which is why he is going to have us bumped off before things start buzzing in the morning.'

'He'll find it difficult to explain his action,' observed Algy.

'What of it? That won't help us. He will say he is very sorry indeed, and all that sort of thing – and then what, as the Americans say? After all, he is a general, and as such must have a good deal of authority. Whether that permits him to carry out capital punishment is another matter, but he has only to say that he is as capable of making mistakes as any one else to end the argument. He may not even have to do that. If he is ready to strike, and I suspect he must be, the Count and Ludwig will have to look out for their own skins.'

'Well, I call it a pretty raw deal,' yawned Algy, tilting the bench back. 'I always did hate the hour of dawn, ever since I was dragged out to fly before it was light in the old days in France. I shall hate it even more in future.'

'Well, you won't have to bear many more,' smiled Biggles.

'I must say I should like to know what Ginger is doing,' muttered Algy. 'Poor kid, he'll be at his wits' end.'

'Don't you believe it,' returned Biggles confidently. 'If you could see him at this moment I'll warrant he's buzzing about like a hornet that has been turfed out of its nest. If they bump us off there will be brick-ends flying in this part of the world until they catch him.'

Algy nodded moodily. 'Do we get breakfast, I wonder?'

'They forgot all about dinner, so I should think it is hardly likely.' Biggles turned an eye to the window. 'Is it my imagination or is the sky beginning to turn grey?' he asked.

'Imagination,' replied Algy shortly, knowing quite well that it was not. 'What about bashing the fellows on the head when they come in to fetch us?' he suggested.

'What with?'

Algy looked around. 'No, there doesn't seem to be much in the way of weapons, does there?' he murmured. 'Pity. I should have liked to knock somebody's scalp off before the play begins – just to hand out a souvenir or two, if you get my meaning. Hark! Do I hear footsteps?'

'You do,' replied Biggles, getting off the table.

'Big, heavy footsteps, like soldiers' boots coming nearer.'

'Oh, shut up.'

'Well, you asked me. Here, I fancy, are the gentlemen in blue.'

A key grated in the lock, and a moment later the door swung open. A warder entered with a lantern. Vilmsky stood on the threshold, in full uniform, his smartness marred by the fact that he had not shaved. Behind him, in the corridor, could be seen a file of soldiers with rifles at the 'order'.

179

'Gentlemen, the time has come,' announced Vilmsky stiffly.

'So I gather,' replied Biggles easily.

Vilmsky stood aside. The soldiers tramped into the cell. Two held cords in their hands, and with these they proceeded to tie the prisoners' wrists. Biggles, knowing that resistance was futile, stood quite still, but Algy would have struggled had not several men held him by the arms and legs.

The operation completed, Vilmsky stepped forward with two handkerchiefs, folded bandage-wise, in his hand.

'What are those for?' asked Biggles politely.

'It is customary to blindfold—'

'Forget it,' Biggles interrupted him curtly. 'I always like to see where I am going.'

Vilmsky bowed. 'As you wish,' he said.

The escort fell in on either side of the prisoners, and at a word of command the party moved forward. Down the corridor it marched, and through an open door into a grim-looking courtyard. Across this it proceeded, and came to a halt against a wall on the far side.

Biggles glanced at the sky. It was just turning pink with the first flush of dawn. 'If Ginger is going to do the rescue act, he hasn't much time left,' he observed calmly.

Algy said nothing. His face was pale.

The soldiers fell in line about twelve paces away. Vilmsky, curiously meticulous, dressed them from the right. Satisfied, he snapped an order, and the rifles came to the 'ready'.

It was at that moment that Biggles heard an aeroplane approaching. He knew by the sound of the engine that it was flying very low, and automatically he raised his eyes. The machine swept into view, and he felt a twinge of disappointment when he saw that it was a strange type.

He noted, too, that it carried the brown crosses of Lovitzna. Vaguely, he had had a fleeting hope that it might be Ginger in one of their machines, although even if it had been it was difficult to see what he could do.

With the order to take aim on his lips, Vilmsky threw a startled glance upwards, almost as if he feared attack, for the noise of the engine as the machine raced low over the enclosed space was deafening; indeed, the aircraft was so low that its wheels skimmed the battlements of the fort. As it swept over the centre of the courtyard something white fluttered down, and struck the ground not ten yards from the firing party.

Vilmsky hesitated, clearly undecided as to whether to proceed with the execution or see what it was the machine had dropped. He looked up again at the aircraft, now banking dangerously, its wing-tip almost touching the wall as it turned. A hand and arm appeared over the side of the cockpit, jabbing downward vigorously. It seemed to decide Vilmsky, who perceived, at any rate, that he had nothing to fear. An order brought the butts of the rifles to the ground again, and he walked quickly to the object that had fallen.

Biggles, watching, saw him remove what appeared to be a piece of string and a weight, both of which he dropped on the ground in order to unfold a sheet of paper to which they had been attached. For what seemed an eternity of time he stood reading the paper, then he thrust it into his pocket and walked back quickly to the firing party.

That was, perhaps, the worst moment of all for the prisoners. Both had been resigned, prepared for the worst, but now a ray of hope had shot into the hearts of both of them.

'I wish he'd do what he's going to do,' snarled Algy. 'I

don't mind being shot, but I hate standing here while that rat reads his morning correspondence.'

'It seems to be vastly interesting, whatever it is,' returned Biggles quietly. 'Ah, he's made up his mind. Now we shall know what it's all about.'

Vilmsky was, in fact, coming towards them, a dour expression on his face. 'You are fortunate,' he said shortly. 'I have an order from General Bethstein countermanding the sentence until he arrives. In the meanwhile, you will return to your cell.'

Again the escort lined up beside the prisoners, who were marched back to their room where the cords were taken from their wrists. This done, the soldiers withdrew. Vilmsky closed the door, and they were left alone.

'Who was it, do you think?' asked Algy breathlessly.

'Ginger.'

'Impossible.'

'I'm not a betting man, but I'd wager what little money I've got to an old tyre that Ginger was flying that machine.'

'What makes you think that?'

'Just a hunch, that's all.'

'Could you see the pilot's face?'

'No. I caught a glimpse of his head as he flashed over, but it was all smothered up with a helmet and goggles.'

Algy sat down heavily. 'What a time we're having,' he said wearily. 'I don't know about you, but I find this messing about worse than flying in a dog-fight with a jammed gun.'

'Yes, it is a bit harrowing,' admitted Biggles, resuming his seat on the table. 'Still, all we can do now is to wait for the next move.'

An anxious half-hour followed, during which time they conjectured on the identity of the mysterious airman.

Then footsteps were again heard approaching down the passage.

'Well, here come the boys in blue again,' smiled Biggles.

But this time he was mistaken. A tense moment while the key turned in the lock, and then the door was flung open violently. Ginger burst in. Behind him were the Count, Ludwig, and several soldiers in uniforms they had not previously seen.

'Hello, everybody,' cried Biggles. 'You don't know how pleased I am to see you.'

Ginger, with an extraordinary expression on his face, sank down on the bench. 'Strewth!' he muttered wearily. 'I'm just about all in.'

'So were we, just now,' Algy told him grimly.

'Come along,' said the Count. 'We can find a more cheerful place than this to talk in, I think.'

Chapter 21

All's Well

'Hello, what's happened here?' Biggles asked the Count, as they emerged from the corridor into the barrack square, where many soldiers in the new uniform were moving about with a brisk air of activity.

'The barracks have been taken over by the Royal Guards. I am in command of the garrison,' replied the Count, leading the way to what had been General Bethstein's private office.

'The deuce you are! What has the general got to say about that?'

'I imagine that the less he says, the wiser he will be,' answered the Count significantly. 'He is under arrest for high treason. With Klein and Zarovitch he has been taken to the civil prison for safe custody.'

Biggles stared. 'Zarovitch! How the dickens did he get here? What's happened?'

Ginger ran over the events of the night for his and Algy's benefit.

'Great Scott!' ejaculated Biggles. 'You certainly have had a time.'

'The biggest shock of the lot came when that hound Bethstein told us that you were due to be shot in half an hour,' went on Ginger. 'I don't mind telling you that I nearly went crazy; there didn't seem to be any way of getting to you in time to save you. Then I remembered the aeroplane that Zarovitch had come over in, still standing out on the field. The Count made Bethstein write an order cancelling his previous instructions by promising that he would hang him on the nearest tree if he refused. And I believe he meant it. The general thought so, too, for he went pretty white about the gills and signed the order as meekly as a lamb. I dashed up to the machine. The pilot had already been arrested, so I grabbed his flying-kit and over I came, sweating with fright for fear of a forced landing or that I might be too late. I had visions, too, of the message falling into a bush or something and not being found. Then I saw you out in the courtyard and the rest was easy. I was watching so hard to see what Vilmsky would do that I nearly hit a chimney.'

'I saw you,' answered Biggles. 'The first rule in the air is to look where you are going.'

'Not having eyes in the back of my head I couldn't look in two places at once, and I had to see what happened to you,' replied Ginger. 'When I was satisfied that you had been taken back inside I went off and landed in a field beside the road, where I waited for the others to come along in the cars. They picked me up, and – well, here we are. You know the rest.'

'Well, laddie, you certainly saved our lives,' declared Biggles seriously. 'Things were looking pretty grim when you appeared.' He turned to the Count. 'And what is the position now with regard to Maltovia?' he asked.

'With Bethstein and Klein where they can do no more mischief, I think we shall soon have the situation in hand. The events of the last few hours will shake Lovitzna, particularly when it is known that Prince Zarovitch—'

'Did you say *Prince* Zarovitch?'

'Yes; didn't you know? Zarovitch is the family name of

the ruling House of Lovitzna. The man you know, Prince Paul, is the king's nephew.'

Biggles slapped his thigh. 'Why, that's grand,' he announced. 'Do you know what I should do if I were you?'

The Count looked up expectantly.

'I'd have a quick trial and sentence all three of those scoundrels to death for espionage and conspiracy. That will make Lovitzna sit up. When she sends a frantic protest, as she is bound to, reply with an ultimatum to the effect that you will hold up proceedings on one condition only, which is that the whole thing be laid before the League of Nations* at Geneva for consideration. They will have to agree to that whether they like it or not, and that will give you plenty of time to get things into shipshape order over here. If Lovitzna does not agree to the League's decision, you will then be ready for anything she cares to start.'

A smile broke over the Count's care-worn face. 'Bigglesworth, I always felt that you should have been a politician,' he said emphatically. 'I am certain of it now.'

Biggles laughed scornfully. 'Me a politician? Not on your life! I'm a soldier.'

'Never mind,' went on the Count quickly. 'The plan you have outlined is our obvious course, so you will forgive me if I leave you now to put it before the new Ministry of Defence without delay. What would you like to do?'

'I would like to go to bed, and sleep and sleep and sleep,' answered Biggles. 'Then I should like to wake up slowly, have a hot bath, and then sit down to a square

* An organization of independent countries which operated from 1920 to 1946. It was replaced by the United Nations (UN).

meal. It seems a long time since I saw either a bed or a proper meal.'

The Count nodded. 'I think that is the best thing you could do. A car shall take you to your hotel right away. When you have done all the things you mention, come up to the palace. Somebody will be anxious to thank you in person. Bring your mechanic with you. By the way, the one who was hurt is out of danger, I hear. We took him to the hospital.'

'That was Carter,' put in Ginger. 'He got knocked on the head. I'll tell you about that later on.'

Algy yawned. 'If we don't soon go somebody will have to carry me,' he declared.

'I'll drive you down,' offered Ludwig, as they moved towards the door.

There is little more to tell. The crisis passed, as Biggles had prophesied, as soon as the Lovitznian government realized into what a dangerous position its prince had placed himself. It accepted the Maltovian ultimatum unconditionally, and the whole case was submitted to the League of Nations, who demanded that all preparations for war should cease while the circumstances were examined.

On the day following the events narrated in the foregoing chapter, the three airmen, with Smyth in attendance, reported at the palace, where they were graciously received by Princess Mariana, who thanked them in terms of sincere regard for what they had done, and with her own hands pinned on their breasts the Maltovian Order of Saint Peter which was the highest decoration the country could bestow. She concluded by asking them to remain in the country until things were quite settled, and to occupy their time by organizing a Royal Air Force on British lines.

187

To this Biggles agreed readily, and his task was made easier when the League of Nations not only issued a verdict in favour of Maltovia, but awarded an indemnity, to be paid by Lovitzna, for what had transpired. A part of this money was allocated to the Air Arm for the purchase of aeroplanes and the training of pilots.

They were still in the country when the forthcoming marriage of Ludwig and his princess was announced, and they were invited to the ceremony. Bethstein and Klein they saw only once again, and that was when they gave evidence at their trial for high treason. They were found guilty and sentenced to death, and in due course met their fate in the very courtyard where Biggles and Algy had so nearly met theirs. Zarovitch was permitted to return to Lovitzna after signing a document to the effect that he would never set foot in Maltovia again.

Their work finished, Biggles at length asked permission to return to his own country, and this was, of course, granted. The occasion was made a bank holiday, for the whole story having been published, they were regarded by the entire nation, rightly perhaps, as the saviours of their country. The procession to the station was in the nature of a Roman triumph, the princess, her consort, and the Count accompanying them on to the platform, where they were the last to shake hands with them.

As the train steamed out of the station to the cheers of the populace Biggles sank back on his seat and lighted a cigarette. 'Well, you fellows, I hope your craving for adventure has now abated somewhat,' he murmured.

'I think we've had enough to go on with for a bit,' agreed Algy.

Ginger smiled. 'Where do we go next?' he inquired.

Biggles shook his head sorrowfully. 'The trouble with some people is that they are never satisfied,' he said sadly.